For those who did not return.

Also by Neil Stanners

'The Magic Room'

'Visions'

'Somewhere Night Falls'

'Assigned Climes'

The Knowing Room

(Der Wissende Raum)

NEIL STANNERS

Published by Garamonde 2020

GARAMONDE

International distribution.
Copyright (Text and Covers) Neil Stanners 2020.
The moral right of the author has been asserted.

Production by Media Services.

ISBN 978-1-86275-015-9

Neil Stanners was born in Sydney.

Spent his time being many things.

He lived and worked in Europe.

He now resides once again in Sydney.

CHAPTERS

DEVELOPMENTS

*In 1939 the German Nazi regime began experimenting with
poison gas as part of their 'Aktion T4' programme of
extermination. Their initial targets were hospital patients.
Those diagnosed as disabled or mentally ill.
These people were labelled Lebensunwertes Leben
(Life Unworthy Of Life).
An idea in which groups were considered a drain on the nation
and had no right to live.
The work was carried out by the SS on Germans then on
Austrians and Poles as the German empire spread.*

*During a visit to the outskirts of Minsk in 1941 to observe mass
shootings, SS Commander Heirich Himmler was told that the
endless execution of prisoners and the local population was
having a bad effect on morale of the SS Einsatzgruppen troops.
It was tiring, costly (a waste of ammunition), a negative use of
resources, slow and inefficient and took troops away from other
duties.*

*Himmler took note this information and immediately began a
quest for a better method of killing large numbers of people.
Initially the 'Aktion T4' method was used. Lethal doses of carbon
monoxide exhaust fumes from banks of petrol engines was fed
into large chambers and the victims eventually succumbed.*

*In late 1941 a deputy at Auschwitz concentration camp tried a
new method. Containers of the crystallised prussic acid known
as Zyklon B (Blausäure) were dropped on prisoners in a sealed
bunker. Once exposed to the air the Zyklon B released amounts
of cyanide gas sufficient to quickly kill all those trapped in
the sealed area. The results were impressive and although
experimentations continued, this new method became the
standard for all Nazi Extermination Camps.*

PART ONE

Chapter 1

'Awakening'

For many days there was nothing. Figures moved about and noise fluttered in and out but this activity was not understood. Time slid past the bed tugging and hovering then moving on. He heard a noise that seemed close. It was his own breath moving in and out like air from an escape valve. Occasionally his fingers might briefly explore the white sheets but the action was involuntary.
They kept him stable. Provided his needs in the way of fluids and care. There was little more to be done.
Drugs kept him motionless, to give time for healing to take place, both physically and mentally. Perhaps also his small stature played a part in his exhausted sleep.

It was the Captain's express wishes, orders in fact, that this boy be given the utmost chance of survival and recovery. Staff did their job. They washed him periodically, tended his

dressings, wiped his brow and soothed him. The doctors
suggested that this young person in the far bed, isolated by
a screen, may have information that the Captain was keen to
obtain. Penicillin had saved him.

After the 'incident', in which this patient was involved, the
whole city of Berlin seemed to have become quiet.
The Germans had taken their last defiant gasp and now, defeated and cowed, they had become more keenly interested
in day to day survival. A task of immense proportions.
Their city was firmly in the control of the Russian Army.
A vengeful lot who were bitter and angry. As the cause of
the incredible suffering of the Russian nation the German
population remained wary and took great lengths to avoid
confrontation or even conversation with their conquerers, if
it could be managed.

On the seventh day some light appeared. Faint flickering
light as he moved his eyelids. It was confusing. An awareness
of blurred shapes and some colours entered his world, Voic-
es, touch, movement all became apparent. His eyes opened
briefly but closed again. He moved a little beneath the bed
sheets.
A discussion took place at his bedside. He was about to be
reunited with reality and wakefulness. The sedatives would
stop. It would take a day for him to slide back to consciousness. The process was to be slow due to a lack of oxygen
supplies.
In the bed, he tried to listen to the ghosts about him.
He thought he heard his name. He knew his name though
little else.

There were others from the 'incident' in nearby beds.
Wounded Russian regular soldiers. They would not speak.
The Captain's assistant, Comrade Kozuch had been to see
each of them the moment they were awake. Whatever had
transpired in the firefight with the SS unit it was forbidden
territory for discussion.
The German soldiers had all been killed. The fight took place
in an apartment building. A high one that could be seen in
the distance from the field hospital.
Civilians must have been involved. Despite their loathing
for the German people, the staff felt a little sorrow for the
German boy. He may have lost his family. Was he an innocent
or one of the crazed children the last days of war had produced?

For the first time since entering the city the Russian troops
could breathe the air without the cloying stench of rotting,
dead bodies in their mouths.
The removal of the dead was tasked to civilians under Russian supervision. Many were buried in makeshift pits in
cemeteries. Attempts were made at identification and photos
were taken where the state of the corpse was such that it
may still assist those searching for missing persons.
The worst streets were sprayed with disinfectant.

Soup kitchens were established to feed the most desperate
though priority was given to the Russian Armed forces.
Engineers worked on establishing a functioning water system in the broken streets. Before setting up standpipes they
needed to trace the water's source to ensure the water was
not contaminated. A great amount of care was taken not to

create an outbreak of sickness or poisoning by infection.
It could destroy any plans to settle some routine and order
in this wrecked world.

His first conscious thought was hunger, followed by confusion. His eyes searched the ceiling and the net wall sur-
rounds. He was in a bed. A lot of his immediate area was
white. His bed was metal. Also white though chipped in
places. The sheets were white and the blanket dark red.
His arm was attached to a tube and a bottle that hung above
the bed on a stand with a hook. With his free arm he felt under the covers. There was bandaging around his torso.
He was wearing just some shorts hitched under his dressings. He moved his legs. Both were still attached to his body.
His mind began to collect pieces of the past. In the apartment. The pain. Lying on the lounge. Feeling so sick. His sav-
iours, his friends talking to him. What did they say? Where
were they?
He attempted to sit up. A sharp pain leapt through his body
from under the bandages.
He gave an involuntary squeak and flopped back on the
pillow.
A head appeared round his screen. She smiled and spoke.
He did not understand what she was saying. Though the
'Ahh" seemed to indicate that she was pleased to see him.
Then she was gone, calling in her foreign language.
Another voice said, "Aha."
Footsteps, then a man appeared.
His words sounded like "Privet moy malen'kiy drug."
He looked closely at the boy's eyes, first one then the other
then took the boy's wrist and consulted his watch. He nod-

ded and said, "Khorosho, Khorosho." He nodded again and held the back of his hand against the boy's neck. Then he tapped the boy's cheek. Then he left.

The boy lay back, exhausted from the little effort he had made. He breathed carefully finding that deep breaths produced pain.

After several minutes a new man appeared. This man was not a nurse or a doctor. He wore a Russian army uniform. He was holding a tray. He spoke German.

"Hullo Hauke. It's good to see you're recovering well. You're no doubt a bit troubled and don't know what is happening. I won't go into lots of details now but to reassure you, all is well. You are in a Russian Army Hospital and we've been looking after you. When you're a bit better we'll talk and help you. Right now I'll get you another pillow, then I'll help you sit up and perhaps you can eat some food. Is that all okay with you?"

Hauke blinked, his mouth hanging open.

"Yes," he said at last, interested at the huskiness of his voice.

Shortly after, propped by a pillow doubled over at his shoulder blades he sat alone with a tray on his lap.

On the tray was a beef sandwich cut into four pieces and a mug of milky tea.

Chapter 2

'Remembering'

For two more days the boy behind the screens was fed and
comforted by the silent but pleasant nursing staff.
The doctor also visited. On the morning of the third day
when he changed the dressing on Hauke's abdomen, the boy
was able to see the red line that had been opened below
his rib cage. Now it had black stitches. They were small and
neat.
He counted them. There were fifteen.
The Russian army man who spoke German came in and had
a conversation with the doctor. They were obviously discussing the boy and his condition. He wondered why they
whispered. Did they think he spoke Russian?
The man in uniform then moved to where Hauke was lying
on his bed. He smiled, tilting his head slightly as if to add to
the friendliness of the occasion.
He pointed to the bandages.

"The doctor says you are doing very well. In a few days they will take the stitches out. He says you will have a scar but due to his nice work, the scar will fade quite a lot in time. He also says you are a very lucky young fellow. The bayonet managed to miss all the vital organs within that part of your abdomen. It was to be internal bleeding that nearly took you away. You got some nice Russian blood. We are a generous people with our blood. You are too young to recognise the bitterness and irony in my remark."

Hauke simply stared at the man in his brown uniform with its red epaulettes. In the silence he added.

"Do you mistrust me?" the man asked.

Hauke looked at the man his eyes unblinking He continued to look while pondering his answer.

"You invaded our country," he said, his fingers drawing nervous circles on the bedsheet, "but I understand that we invaded yours. I don't understand war or why it happens. You saved my life and you are all being very nice. The war is over now. I don't know what will happen next. I have nobody but Adriane and Dieter. I will trust you if you can tell me where they are? Can they come for me?"

The Russian sat on the bed. He patted the boy's knee.

"I'm sorry, you must be very anxious but please understand, a war has finished, now the real work begins. There is so much to do. To make things right again. You were in the military. I suppose you were also in the Hitler Youth?"

"Everybody was in the Hitler Youth. It was compulsory."

"Ah, of course. Did you kill many of our soldiers when in battle."

The boy looked abashed.

"I didn't fire my gun. I was too scared. I just ran away. They tried to shoot me.”

“Who? Our Russian soldiers?”

“No, our commander. But then he died so he couldn’t shoot any more of us.”

The Russian paused.

“I see,” he said. “Yes, that happens. Although Russia does not use children to fight their wars.”

He raised his hands as in appeal.

“Hauke, look upon me as a messenger. Tomorrow when you can walk about, we’ll get you out of this bed and we’ll go together to see Captain Chaban, the head of this sector. We will ask you a lot of questions about the apartment you were hiding in. There will be no right or wrong answers. You are not in trouble, we are simply interested in the man who owned that apartment and we want to know anything you can tell us about your time there.”

“You mean Dr Beck?”

“Yes, that’s him.”

“Are you going to kill him?”

“No, no, quite the opposite. He is a very clever man. A scientist. We would like him to help us, to share his knowledge. It is what scientists do. First we have to locate him. He may have died in the war, we don’t know but we can help him.”

Hauke looked at his visitor. The man was a little unnerved. Beneath his untidy blonde hair the boy had quite piercing golden-brown eyes.

“Then I will be of no further use to you.”

From his training in Army Intelligence, the Russian had the right answer.

“If you help us and tell us all you know I give you my word we will do our best to find these people you mentioned and

help you meet again. Is that a fair deal, my young friend?”
The boy looked again. There was an overwhelming sadness
in his face, his body, his demeanour. The Russian had seen
it many times before, in the endless processions of crushed,
lost people who stretched across Europe. All using hope as
their last refuge against reality. The American soldiers had
given it a name. They called it the ‘1000 yard stare.’ However, it was not his job to feel pity.
He stood and patted the boy’s shoulder.
“Till tomorrow then. I’ll see if I can find some cake to have
with the tea.”
He made to leave and then stopped. Against his better judgment, he spoke again.
“I have a son Hauke. He’s the same age as you. I understand.
That is why I won’t let you down.”

As he left the man from the NKVD tried to convince himself
that his last statement was part of the strategy for befriending prisoners in order to win their confidence and extract
information.

Chapter 3

'The Meeting'

The Russians had found him a new shirt and shorts. The
shirt was blue and a little too big. He wore the same boots
and socks he had been wearing when the 'incident' took
place.
As he entered the Captain's upstairs office he noted there
was a large pot of tea on the desk and also a good-sized plate
of cake.
Captain Chaban was a big man. He was seated on the edge of
his desk and rose when Hauke entered with his minder.
The captain walked over to the boy taking his hand and
shaking it warmly.
"Hello Hauke, it's good to meet you and to see you well
again. My name is Captain Chaban."
He motioned to another man in the room.
"This is my most trusted assistant Comrade Kozuch. Please
sit down here. It's a particularly nice day outside. Let's have

some tea and cake and we'll talk."

Hauke sat in the little group, holding a plate with two pieces of cake and a mug of tea poured by Comrade Kozuch. The cake tasted of orange. It even had cream icing. Captain Chaban sat in front of him their knees almost touching. The other Russian army man sat beside him. Even Comrade Kozuch pulled up a chair. Several thoughts went through the boy's mind. The cake was delicious, all three men in the room spoke excellent German and the man next to him had never told him his name.

The Captain finished his cake and licked the tips of fingers.
"I did enjoy that," he said.
He looked at the small figure in front of him.
"Right Hauke. Let's begin. Are you comfortable? No pain from your wound?"
"No, it doesn't hurt."
"Good, good. Keep eating your cake. There's more if you want it. Though do not make yourself sick. Now, I'll start by telling you everything I know about you. Which is not a lot. Then you can tell me if I'm right.
Is that acceptable?"
The boy nodded.
The Captain noticed his eyes but held his gaze.
"We became aware of the building you were in when gunfire from your building began hitting our canteen just down the road from here. A number of our soldiers were wounded. We immediately sent some troops to your building to investigate. Inside we encountered some members of your SS soldiers who were ready to die it would seem. The building

was very difficult to access but of course you know that.

A fight took place as we advanced up the stairs floor by floor until we reached the top floor. Our soldiers, I might add, assumed that the building was empty, due to the bomb damage to one side.

When our soldiers chased the last two SS men to your apartment and entered, they found both men dead on the floor. Then somebody shot at them. Two of my three men fell.

The man shooting stopped. His gun was empty. As my soldier advanced a figure leapt out at him bearing a knife.

That figure Hauke was you. In a natural reflex my soldier bought up his bayonet and it caught you in the stomach. You fell to the floor. I might add that my soldier was deeply concerned that he had wounded a boy.

The man who had been firing from behind a lounge attacked my remaining soldier bringing him down and beating him unconscious.

It was then that one of my wounded soldiers watched two people, the man and a woman who had also been behind the lounge, lift you onto the lounge. They were deeply distressed and talked to you. Apparently, you said something to them but then you fell silent. I assume the man and the woman are these people you call Adriane and Dieter."

Captain Chaban looked at Hauke. The boy's eyes were full of tears as he nodded. He placed his hand on the boy's shoulder. He continued, his voice low.

"Please bear with me. You're being very brave. These people sat with you for a while but it was obvious they were anxious to leave. The reasons too were obvious. They rose, they kissed your cheek, they stopped and tended briefly to my wounded men then they left, making them comfortable.

We are sure that the only reason they left you, Hauke, was that they thought you had died.

A short time later reinforcements from my troops arrived and after examining the building they sent word that I should come to look at the apartment.

There were so many interesting aspects to this building and its contents. First, the fact that it was standing at all with the side blown out. Then our engineers pointed out that it was constructed around a central core. The cleverness of your enterprise to find your way into the building despite the large section of missing stairwell and the presumably good fortune that you found an apartment at the top that was stocked with food and had both water and gas still operating. It must have been quite wonderful for you."

"We called it The Magic Room," said Hauke.

"Pardon."

"We called the apartment, The Magic Room. We were very lucky."

Chaban paused and nodded.

"Yes, I suppose you were. There was not a lot of luck about in your city. Now we're coming to the end of my bit of this story. Soon you will have to take over. What we also discovered was that this apartment you were occupying was the apartment of Dr Antek Beck who as my comrade here has discussed with you, is a scientist with whom we would be delighted to share ideas and knowledge.

At first, we thought that the man who had left might have been Dr Beck but we decided that it could not be so as he was working a long way away and had not been reported near Berlin for some time. We only know your first name because our wounded man heard these people call you by it.

You have called these people Adriane and Dieter.

So, in summary, you and some other people spent a lot of time in an apartment belonging to Dr Beck. Why and how? Did you know him? Did you ever meet him? Are any of you related to Dr Beck? Who are Adriane and Dieter? Are they your parents? What is your connection with Dr Beck?"

The Captain held up his hand.

"Now we're going to stop and have some more tea and cake. I want you to understand Hauke that whatever you tell us you are not in any trouble nor are Adriane and Dieter or Dr Beck. We mean none of you any harm. And, I will help you as much as I can if you're truthful with me."

Bending down Chaban took the boy by the chin and gently lifted his head. He raised his eyebrows.

Hauke looked at him. He could not help it, he liked the man. He also liked Comrade Kozuch. It was just a feeling he had.

"Yes," he said, "I understand."

The cake was just as delicious the second time and the fresh tea still hot from the samovar.

Kozuch took Hauke to the windows.

"This was an inn. I suppose it will be again someday. It has a nice kitchen downstairs. We have almost as much food as you did in your Magic Room." He smiled and the boy smiled back. "In fact we brought a lot of the food back here. That Dr Beck must have decided to throw lots of big parties but he seems not to have had the chance."

Seated once again in front of the Captain the man said, "Right, let's begin with the most important question. Who are Adriane and Dieter? You can answer all my other questions as you go. Now take a deep breath."

Hauke did take a deep breath but then began to cry quietly. After half a minute he took another deep breath and began to talk.

"My name is Hauke Kluge. Adriane and Dieter are not my parents. They are my friends, my new family. They said we'd start a new life together. We were going to leave Berlin and go to the country." He hesitated.

"You were going to try to get to the American zone weren't you?"

Hauke looked shocked but then nodded.

"It's okay. It does seem a wish for some Germans. They don't like us. Are you an orphan Hauke?"

Tears rolled down the boy's face.

"My parents were killed in the bombing, my brother was killed in army, my relatives are all dead."

"And Dieter and Adriane?"

Dieter was soldier in the Wermacht. His parents were killed in Dresden.

Adriane lived on a farm. She watched from a field as Russian troops did horrible things to her family and then murdered them all. She ran to Berlin to hide."

A silence fell over the room. Kozuch cleared his throat. They waited.

Finally, the captain said, " None of us have much to be proud of in this terrible conflict. Please go on when you're ready."

The boy sipped some tea. He seemed to have shrunk on his chair as if weighed down by the burden of his memories. Kozuch decided to help.

"Tell us, Hauke, how did you three lost souls all meet?"

Here was a question that was easy to answer.

"It started with Adriane," he said. "She was trying to find somewhere to hide, to be safe. She realised the building was strong and climbed up the walls to get to the staircase."

"What, no ladders?"

"No."

"I am impressed. Please continue."

The boy looked up, twisting his fingers in the anguish of the next part of his story.

"It was me who came next. I was a Hitler youth soldier. We were overrun near the railway junction. Only a few of us escaped. I found a ladder resting against the landing in the building so I climbed it then ran up the stairs to near the top. I was asleep in one of the empty apartments when the man who had put the ladder up came back. He was SS. He was planning to shoot Russians from the balcony. When he saw me he began yelling and called me a deserter and a coward. He got some rope and made me stand on a table. He was about to hang me when Adriane came to the door and shot him dead."

The boy swallowed hard and began to cry again his shoulders shaking. But he continued his story.

"She was so kind, so nice. She took me upstairs bathed my neck. She gave me food. She told me I'd be safe and that she would look after me from now on. I love Adriane very much."

The three men listening were intrigued and touched by this tale of desperation.

"How did Dieter arrive?" asked Chaban.

"He just appeared at the door one afternoon. He had run away from any more fighting."

"What was he wearing?" asked Chaban suddenly.

The boy sensed a trap. The man they were discussing had been in a Russian uniform. He would not have acquired it by accident. He would never tell Hauke why or what had happened. This part of the story was best left out."

"Civilian clothes. He had taken off his Wehrmacht uniform. He said he was finished with killing and being killed. Dieter was kind and helpful. We were all going to start a life together."

He stopped. Looked round at his questioners.

"Then it all went wrong. I'm alone again."

"Hauke," said Chaban, "We do understand. Don't despair. Who knows what might be possible. Now concentrate, I have to ask you. Please answer carefully. Did any of you know or see or hear from Antek Beck?"

The boy considered for some seconds.

"I'm sorry, no, we didn't know him or know of him. We were just so glad of his apartment. I ...."

"Is there something else Hauke?"

"There's two things. I would sometimes sneak onto our apartment's balcony to look down. I'd lay flat so that I could peer over the edge. To watch what was happening. Dieter told me never to do it in case I was seen but I was curious. One day when I looked over there was a man across the street. He was looking up, directly at our balcony. I think he saw me. I ran inside."

"When did this happen?"

"Not long after we were together."

Captain Chaban looked at the other soldier. The silent man who had first spoken to Hauke. They nodded then the man leaned forward and held a photograph in front of Hauke."

"Is this the man you saw?"

The boy looked for only a second.

"Yes, that's him. I'm certain."

"Well Hauke, that is Antek Beck. What do you suppose he wanted? I mean what a risk he was taking in Berlin days before our army conquered your city."

Hauke Kluge, Hitler Youth soldier and orphan was sure he knew and he felt confident with his answer.

"I think he might have wanted his notebook."

"What notebook is that Hauke?"

"You must have seen it in the apartment. It has a black leather case and is full of notes and scribble and drawings. It had a whole list of addresses in the back."

The three men were all looking at each other. They had found a great deal of general items in the apartment, but no scientific material or research papers nor any 'addresses.'

"You're sure it was there? You saw it?"

"Yes, most definitely. I used to look at it and try to work out what all the writing meant."

The boy was sure he had seen the notebook. He was also sure they would not find it. He had seen Adriane slip it into her bag when they were ready to leave. He had liked the notebook and she must have been going to surprise him with it.

He loved Adriane for her kindness.

While the men in the room discussed this development and the boy sat coyly aware of his cleverness he suddenly realised that he may have put Adriane and Dieter in danger. Now that these men knew about the notebook they might be searching for his friends. He felt sick with worry.

The talk continued for a little longer but it seemed the boy would be of little more use.

Eventually, he was escorted by the nameless officer back to his bed in the hospital.

The man said, "I'd like to thank you Hauke for all your help. We do appreciate your honesty. Hopefully, we will find Dr Beck and we can help him with his work. That would be nice wouldn't it."

Hauke flopped onto his bed. He was tired. Then he wished he had not. He felt a sting from his wounded stomach.

"Will you be coming back tomorrow?"

"I'm not sure," the man said. "Someone will be here to talk about your welfare."

Chapter 4

'An Arrangement'

In his office, Captain Chaban sat at his desk in earnest discussion with Comrade Kozuch.
"I sensed some hesitations. He left some things out. Probably just trying to protect Dieter Falke. The man who injured some of my men. We should have arrested him when we saw him that day. But it's too late now. Perhaps we were being too kind. War is complicated."
"Does he know where the notebook is located?"
Chaban leaned back. He screwed his face up in mock puzzlement.
"Here's the thing about interrogation. The little I know anyway. You have to look at the answers from all sides.
So, does this notebook exist at all or is it just something the boy invented to be helpful? There was a little of the 'lost treasure aspect to the story. If it exists could one of our men have taken it as a souvenir? Could it still be in the apart-

ment? Another search is probably required. I doubt this Adriane and Dieter would have taken it with them. They didn't need any extra weight and I'd imagine it would have seemed of no importance. "

The man from Army Intelligence returned.
"Back in his bed?" asked Chaban.
"Yes. Looks a little lost."
"I'll consider his future tomorrow. Now you're here, any observations from the talk?"
The man smiled and raised his hand, forefinger extended.
"Ah, yes. One stood out. That boy definitely saw Beck outside in the street. His reaction to the photo said it all. As if I had vindicated his information by showing him a photo he recognised. Considering the timing of the event I suspect Antek Beck may be close by, comrades. Somewhere in this sector. He will be seen sooner or later. If we get him, a missing notebook will be of little consequence. Having the mind of one of the leading Peenemunde rocket men in our fold will do wonders for the motherland."

Some weeks after this discussion in Berlin. Adriane Gerst and Dieter Falke were able to cross into the US-controlled zone in Hesse in Southern Germany. They were interrogated at an Army base at Bad Hersfeld. With the help of information obtained from a notebook that Adriane presented to the US authorities the scientist, Antek Beck was captured staying at a friend's house. The address had been found in the back of the notebook. This news was not released by the US Army until Dr Beck and his family were transported to the US mainland

In the morning as Comrade Kozuch brought his Captain a
cup of coffee and some bread rolls he commented, "You have
been thinking Captain, I can tell."

"I have Comrade, I have. I know what I'm going to do with the
boy."

"I'm intrigued. What are you going to do with him?"

"Employ him, that's what I'm going to do with him. We have
spare rooms on this floor, don't we? This was an inn after all.
I know our friend from the NKVD has left us but I think
there might be a little more young Hauke can tell us. He's an
innocent but he is also alone and he must be frightened for
his future. If he's close by and we get to know him then there
might be some morsel of information we can garner that was
previously unavailable."

Kozuch sipped his coffee. It was a tradition that the two had
developed in having their breakfast together.

"I must admit I did consider that our man from NKVD may
have taken him aside and shot him. It is their normal course
of action when dealing with a German prisoner for which

they have no further use."

Chabin glanced at Kozuch.

"I wondered that myself. I considered whether it would be a foolish move to try to prevent such an occurrence. It seems the man has children of his own. I think our boy reminded him of one. So perhaps not all our NKVD people are so ruthless though their reputation does little to quell such notions. What do you think of my idea Comrade?"

"It's a sound idea Captain. Can we trust him? He is German. His country is ruined and he's alone. Who knows where his resentments or loyalties may lie. He could have murderous intent. What he told us of his time as a soldier seemed plausible but it may be untrue."

The Captain leaned back and squinted at the window.

"Yes, I hear what you say but I don't see a fanatic. I see a lost child. I watched him talk. I did not see a glint of zealous patriotism. He didn't fight to the death in his first and only skirmish, he turned tail and ran. No greater glory there, just self-preservation. His own people murdered his friends and tried to murder him. I can't see there's any loyalty to any cause. He just wants to survive and find some happiness. I'd like to try this idea out for a while."

Kozuch nodded.

"The immediate staff here don't seem to mind him so I see no conflict there. I'll seek out a nice room with a sunny aspect and try to make it a little comforting for a twelve-year-old."

"By the way," added Chaban. "As the go-between in this ruse, I expect he will see more of you. Be his friend, he could no doubt use one at the moment."

"Do you think he has any chance of finding those people he

was with?"

"I doubt it but I'll make inquiries. Even our Army Intelligence man had sympathies for him so the least we can do is try."

Chapter 5

'The Farm'

The day was warm. Dieter stood looking out of his window.
Green shoots were visible in his fields.
He turned to his wife as she entered the room.
"Each day, they are getting bigger. I wish I could hurry them
along."
Adriane stepped up beside the man to look.
"Perhaps they don't like being watched so much."
Dieter kissed Adriane's cheek.
"I want to be successful at this. Kindness from our neigh-
bours has kept us alive, kept us hopeful, taught us rudimen-
tary farming, supplied a dress and a suit, a priest, a church
and our wedding celebration. If I show them I am a fairly
good farmer and a stout reliable neighbour and friend then
their efforts will not have been fruitless."
Adriane looked up at the man next to her. She stepped forward and looked round at his face.

"I have married an old-fashioned man with ethics. A rare commodity in this country of late."

Dieter was about to laugh then the import of her words made sense and he stopped.

For three months they had occupied their new home. Given to them by the US Government in some sort of arrangement with local authorities after the owners were all killed in the war.

The initial strangeness of occupying another person's home had faded and they slowly felt as if they belonged. Items of a personal nature from the previous occupiers were removed and placed in the small cellar. Not a lot remained, perhaps pilfered by people nearby. In such tough times, it would be only natural.

Their immediate neighbours were all older and seemed to have adopted them as an interesting project.

Their generosity both materially and in spirit helped ease the pain of their losses of family and the raw memories of Berlin. The farmers too had suffered and lost children to the rise and fall of Germany's massive folly. Now everybody made an effort to stop being sad and see out each new day. Dieter and Adriane considered themselves luckier than most. Very few Germans had not suffered great tragedy. At least they had each other, they had a home and a fair chance of a decent life ahead. Many others had nothing and nobody.

At their breakfast, they sat eating a little bread with lard and drinking watery coffee. It was warm and filled them.

"Tomatoes soon," said Dieter, "and more potatoes."

Adriane smiled slightly. She just said, "Umm."

Their daily routine was established. They had poultry which they tended carefully and enjoyed the small supply of eggs. On the advice of the nearest neighbour Egon, their fields were planted with food crops. First feed yourself was his philosophy. They would have a lot of cabbages and corn plus beets, some legumes even pumpkins. All in the fullness of time.

Each day in some stage of their conversation they would somehow bring up the subject of Hauke Kluge, the dear, dead boy they were forced to leave behind on the lounge in their 'magic room' apartment.
The memory of him and the circumstances of their parting haunted their lives. He was with them in thought and deed. How he would have loved the farm, the farm life, how he could have helped, what joy, wonder and amusement they would have taken from his chatter and his observations. He may have made friends. There was Manfred the sixteen-year-old, bookish son of the pig farmer over the hill. One gate past Egon was the home of the Muller family. They had a young boy, Lambert, aged just six. A gift, after the others who had waved goodbye in their smart uniforms and were not seen again. Then there was their daughter Mila. A sweet, reserved, yet tough young girl whose age almost exactly matched that of Hauke.
This knowledge added more to their endless sorrow about the boy they lost.

Chapter 6

'Duties'

Kozuch was aware of his door opening. Footsteps on the boards.

"I brought you a hot drink," whispered Hauke. "It's tea I think."

Kozuch blinked, sat up in his bed and looked at the cup in the boy's hand. He took it and tasted it. Then he grunted.

"Yes, it's tea."

He glanced at his watch. Early reddish light came through the window.

"I couldn't sleep," said Hauke, as a way of explanation.

The boy sat on the bed.

"Is the tea pleasant for you?"

"It's nice but so is sleep. You haven't woken the Captain have you?"

"No, I'm not that brave. If I get up early I go and try to talk to the cooks downstairs. They're always up. I don't think they sleep at all. Russian is a strange language. I don't understand much of it."

"Why are you barefoot and wearing parts of a Russian uniform?"

"They took my shorts and shirt and said they needed to wash them. The little cook gave me some of her uniform till my clothes are dry."

Kozuch smiled. For a member of the loathsome Germans who had laid waste to his country and slain so many of his people, he had still been won over by the boy's innocent charm and his efforts to please. Hauke had managed to learn a small list of Russian words and with his need to help wherever possible he had even tamed the often angry kitchen staff and convinced Captain Chaban of his total lack of guile. Neither Kozuch nor the Captain had gained any more knowledge of the events in the apartment. After three months Antek Beck continued to elude them and suspicions grew that the Americans may already have the man in their collection of ex-Nazi scientific hierarchy.

Kozuch almost wished the boy was somehow objectionable because if their attempts to reunite him with the missing Adriane and Dieter were fruitless, they would have to eventually hand him over to a local German orphanage. It would be a sad day if this occurred. The future for such flotsam of the war would be quite miserable he imagined but the Russian Army would not be here forever and the boy needed to return to school and to some sort of life in his community.

"I'll make some inquiries and see if I can't obtain some more clothes for you. Forgive me for not noticing that you only had the one set. You must have washed them before? What did you wear then?"

"I washed them myself and hung them out my window then stayed in my bed till they dried. I'm not very good at washing. This time they will be washed properly."

"You're nothing if not enterprising Hauke. While I'm dressing can you go to check if the captain is up yet? If he is you can take him his breakfast."

"But you always do that. Then you sit and talk."

"Well for today let's have a change. I note you are not wearing shoes?"

"They fell to pieces."

"It seems my first order of the day will be to visit the supply clerk and see what can be done for you."

Kozuch watched the boy leave and gently close the door. He gave a snort. If the lad was in fact 'employed' by the Russian Army then technically he should have received some payment for his work. Though the current turmoil did not make for a stable economy. The Reichsmark was massively inflated and untrusted. Allied Occupation Notes were not freely available so the country existed on a mix of money, barter, free enterprise and luck.

Paying rubles would make even less sense.

It was a problem for another day.

After dressing Kozuch made his way to the Captain's office. Chaban was sipping coffee as he entered.

"I thought you had deserted me, Comrade," he said. "Young Hauke has already brought our breakfast. Then I reasoned that you wanted me to see the barefoot pile of rags in his make-do uniform. Next, you're going to tell me that your first order of business will be to find some new clothes for the young fellow."

Kozuch took a seat and picked up a buttered roll and a hard-boiled egg.

"We know each other so well."

Chapter 7

'Balance'

Five Russian regulars from one of the better occupation units
had murdered three German women in their apartment.
The details of their misdemeanour and what they had done
to these women were shocking even to Captain Chaban.
He sat slumped at his desk reading the pages of text. His
mind wandered from the crimes on the papers in front of him
to the delicacy of the reaction he must take. The five perpetrators were locked in a room at the barracks.

Their deeds may not have been traced back to them except
that two German families in the same apartment block had
decided on risking terrible consequences and had spoken up
about what they saw and heard. By luck they had spoken to
a Russian junior officer who felt the Motherland was being
tainted by the monstrous crimes of the Russian occupiers
and thus the report had been prepared and placed before

Chaban for his appraisal.

Kozuch explained that the officer was religious and he wished these men be punished severely to create an example and force the Russian forces in the area to rise above the barbaric revenge tactics they employed on German citizens. "Are we trying to prove that we are a more vile race of people than the Germans. It seems we are."

Strong, brave words for a junior officer. He continued his summary by pointing out that the Russian forces were ruining any chance they had of proving how they were a moral, God-fearing race while the Germans with their acts of state-inspired, unspeakable brutality and their death camps were a sub-human branch of humanity not fit to walk among us.

Chaban rubbed his forehead. This young officer would have been well-advised not have made his point with such zeal. Comrade Stalin and most of his hierarchy of generals and intelligence underlings were not fond of religious tendencies. It was the state that came first. Other potential power bases were a threat. Hence Mother Russia's quiet but ongoing campaign against the church.

In balance, the degree of rape, murder, looting and mayhem that Russian forces had inflicted on the Germans had gone well beyond revenge and had become accepted by most officers as part of their strategy as they swept through Poland and on into the heart of Germany.

The sheer terror of the ill-disciplined, Russian hordes no doubt aided the triumphs over the crumbling German army. Now, with Germany defeated the blood-lust had to stop. Various commanders, Rokossovky, Kopelev, Zhukov and others had all spoken of putting an end to such activity and introducing severe penalties for any transgressors. Russia was now an occupying force. It had work to do in settling the situation, providing stability and establishing working lines of communication, services, food and most of all 'order'. Berlin, in particular, was to be run with efficiency and calm, to demonstrate the quality of the Russian race and Russian forces.

Captain Chaban called to the kitchen for some food and some tea. He was not hungry. Kozuch would bring the tray and he wished to have the man's wise counsel without allowing others in his command, a chance to gossip.

With both men seated, sipping tea, Chaban slid the report across to his adjutant.
"I don't wish to put you in a position in which you feel uncomfortable Comrade but I wonder if you have heard any talk amongst the staff and enlistments about this matter?" Kozuch looked at Chaban. He put his hand to his mouth briefly. He remained silent for some seconds.
"It is well known and widespread. It is the main topic of conversation. There is little chance it could be quietly put aside. Also, the officer who filed the report is agitating for some action. He wants an example made. I fear he may be overstepping the mark and his career may be in jeopardy but I must tell you Comrade Captain everybody is waiting for your judgement in the matter.."
"I see," said Chaban. "I will not ask for your opinion, that would be cowardly. But as friends rather than members of the Russian armed forces I can only say that this situation worries me greatly. The degree of my decision could have

'consequences' for our whole sector. I'm only a Captain, thrust into this commanding role by circumstance. I realise my position is thus delicate. If I overreact it may be resented. Will I be seen as weak if I do not provide an example?

Kozuch ran his finger around the rim of his cup.

"I'm not sure this will help but I did seek out similar situations that have occurred recently. In the western sector, Markov had two members of the Ukrainian brigade shot for the rape and murder of two girls. It may not be relevant. The victims were only fourteen.

A sergeant in the General Industrial Division staff, they're the ones shipping all the German factories back to our Motherland, was looting a German apartment when the family returned home. They protested so he shot them all.

A woman, her son of eighteen and two ten -year-old cousins. Twins, a boy and a girl. He did not shoot the woman's twenty-one-year-old daughter. He raped her for several hours then slit her throat. No action was taken. Of course these are only the isolated cases that were actually recorded.

I have no information from the British or Americans with regard to similar cases."

Kozuch shrugged.

"So, if you wish to use precedents in your decision …… we find only confusion."

At 12 midday on the following day, the ringleader of the rape and murder group was taken from his cell to the barracks square. His hands were tied and his legs bound together at the knees. Hobbled into position against a wall he was then blindfolded and immediately executed by five riflemen from the Captain's own brigade.

Captain Chaban had made a short announcement beforehand advising that this behaviour was no longer tolerated
and that the Russian army had been advised that such activity would be met with suitable discipline. Rape, terrorising
and murder of the population deserved punishment and for
the culprits, it would be carried out.
Kozuch stood at his side. It was the least he could do.

The four other perpetrators were to be held while a decision
was made on their future.

As Chaban stepped inside following the execution he noticed
a shaking bundle slumped in a corner. It was the boy.
"Hauke," he said, "Did you just witness what happened in the
yard'?
The boy nodded.
"Then come with me. We must talk."
He lifted the boy to his feet. Rather than take his hand he
bade the boy follow him to his office.

Together with Comrade Kozuch he sat Hauke down and
looked at him. Would it be appropriate to give the child a
hug?
"You have seen death before Hauke. The war took over our
lives. Death is much a part of these events. Terrible things
took place but it had to end and it did. Now with our best
efforts working toward restoring a degree of civility, that
man in the yard carried out some awful crimes. He deserved
his punishment. We have just come to the end of this war
Hauke but the peace is almost as difficult as was the conflict beforehand. Please put this behind you. Not long ago

you were our enemy. Now, with the war ended there is no point in being enemies. Of course, these events will not be forgotten but I remind myself that not all Germans knew or understood what they were doing or why. Especially twelve-year-old-boys."

Captain Chaban held out his hand. The boy stood slowly then sniffed, stepped forward and took the Russian's hand. Chaban gave in and pulled the boy into his arms. After a few seconds, he held him at arm's length and said, "Now go to your room and rest. I'll see if we can find you some tea and bread."

Kozuch watched Hauke leave.

"He'll be alright. I'll go to him in a minute. Nobody saw you hug a German boy, so all is well."

Captain Chaban placed his hands on his desk and let out a deep sigh.

"Ah Comrade, I shot one of those criminals. A Russian soldier. One of our own. The others are on hold. I've filed a report. Now we will wait. Word will spread. Others out of my realm and out of my control will decide whether my actions were correct, incorrect or of no consequence. Whatever it brings, the next few days will be interesting."

Chapter 8

'Changes'

For the next week the sector under the control of Captain Chaban seemed quiet. Routines continued. An unsolvable problem with sewerage in a number of streets was suddenly solved by sending some German engineers into the main tunnels to look for a cause.
The men were forced to enter the underground maze. When they returned they asked for a small amount of explosive. It seemed the carcases of some dead horses had choked up the whole system at a large tunnel junction. Russian engineers were reluctant to supply the explosives but after considering the alternative, of entering the sewerage system themselves they acquiesced.
A small crowd waited at the sewerage entry point for some time. Finally there was a substantial 'whump' sound from below and then a rushing sound.
Immediately afterward the two Germans emerged from

underground covered in putrid muck. The crowd dispersed
their hands to their faces.
The German engineers announced that the sewerage was
now clear. They were supplied with two large barrels of
water and told to wash. Their distress was so great that they
were then given some precious bars of soap. They stripped
naked in the street and spent the next quarter hour cleaning
their bodies. Despite threats, they refused to have anything
more to do with their clothes and demanded new attire.
Given some old blankets, they were sent home.

Comrade Kozuch entered the Captain's office at 2.30pm.
He held a fat brown envelope.
The Captain was at the window.
"What's the commotion Comrade?"
"It seems the sewerage problem we were having is no longer
a problem. Some dead horses were moved on."
Chaban turned smiling.
"Well that's something in the form of progress I suppose.
I should get out, do a small tour. Though judging from the
odour even at this distance it may be prudent to wait for
another day."

Over the past week, the Captain had been asking Kozuch for
indications as to the mood of the troops and officers regarding to his decision to execute the rapist and murderer.
Sympathies were running at 60% in favour to 40% against.
Even hardened veterans of the conflict were appalled at the
foul details of the crime. This had swayed many to rethink
their standards and ethics.
Still executing one of their own was a step into an unknown

abyss. Gossip hinted at some form of reaction. The majority who liked the Captain were worried that he may suffer some retribution.

Captain Chaban walked back to his desk.
"What have you brought me, Comrade?"
Kozuch held out the envelope.
"This just arrived by dispatch rider."
Chaban looked at the envelope.
"Oh. This may be the answer to the question."
The adjutant continued to hold out the envelope.
"If I refuse to take it I will never know. That might be the wisest move."
Kozuch put the envelope into his Captain's hand.
"No special detachment has arrived to arrest you, Comrade Captain besides this may simply be a regular update on supplies, logistics, treatment of stray dogs or an invitation to a city briefing."
Chaban broke open the top of the envelope and slid out the papers inside. He motioned to Kozuch.
"Please, join me, Comrade. Whatever the information, news or events contained herein it will be good to have somebody close at hand with whom to discuss their import."

For several minutes Captain Chaban read his way through the pages of material in his hands. He stroked his chin at one stage, shook his head, gave several grunts, cleared his throat and at the end said, "My God."
Then he placed all the pages on his desk, sat back and said again, "My God."
He seemed lost in thought. Finally, he turned to Kozuch and

placed his hands squarely on his desk.

"It's from Wunsdorf. As high as we get I believe. So not a selection of administration figures. They have noted my handling of the case of the torture, rape and mutilation of three German women and after some consideration, they feel my response was justified. They have however requested that the remaining prisoners not be executed but be handed over to our military police. Arrangements will be made shortly for their transfer.

It seems Comrade that rape and looting and even murder are still okay but mutilation is not acceptable."

Kozuch stirred.

"Well, you seem to have survived the ordeal so the news is welcome. I'm confused by your reaction. You said 'My God' twice. That seemed an odd phrase to use when reading what is, after all, a routine piece of correspondence. Is there more?"

Captain Chaban smiled. He reached across and placed his hand on his confidant's shoulder.

"Ah, my dear friend. Yes, there is more news. Somewhat disturbing news. I fear our days together may be numbered."

In the pause that followed Chaban's face was quite benign, as if his thoughts had left the room and floated away from the whole city and the situation.

"What is it, Captain?"

Chaban returned his eyes to Kozuch. He held up the last two sheets of paper.

"Our present rather quiet and largely uneventful existence could not last forever. After all, Europe is mostly in turmoil. It was bound to catch up with us. Here read them for yourself.

Before you do however I must point out that I have mentioned your name in several of my recent official reports.
I may have said some flattering things about you and your abilities. It seems they have taken note."
Kozuch stared at the papers. He reread some sections mouthing the words for clarity.
Then, at last, he said, "My God. This is troubling.
A Major-General Gabitov no less, will be calling by in two days to perform a brief ceremony. You have been promoted to Colonel.
I am to be a Senior Lieutenant. They say I will be assuming responsibility for this sector and you are to be reassigned."
"Yes, that is indeed what they say."
Chaban looked about the room. His room in a small building in a small part of Berlin. He had grown fond of it all.
"Our plans for remaining somewhat anonymous and seeing out the war and the peace in obscurity seem to have come undone."
"I wonder how much time we have left?"

Chapter 9

'The Orphan'

The Russian administration it seemed now moved with some
efficiency and immediacy. All arrangements for the change-
over were to be completed in one week.
Colonel Chaban was to report to Zhukov's Army Group headquarters to command a large unit dealing with transport and
distribution. It would require all his skills in the management
of resources and people.
With little chance for a relaxed handing over of the mantle,
Chaban insisted that Senior Lieutenant Kozuch immediately
move to his office and take charge of the sector acting as if
he were no longer available for guidance.
"It's the best I can do Comrade. A quick course in the many
details of running this place. While I am still here to make
suggestions if needed. You have been doing half of this work
already. You are well-liked and you have the respect of the
men and women in this area. If your life is to be easy then I

suggest you urgently search the ranks and find a Sergeant who can be your adjutant. I propose that you will never find one of your calibre. One who has been as good as you have been to me but if you choose wisely you will at least have a reliable person who will make your job a little less onerous."

The two men spent the first day of their last week together discussing work, the Russian Armed Forces, the future and the past.
"You know," said Kozuch, at one point, "Let us make a pact. I've seen the way you look at this little inn. It has become a retreat for you, a home, a place of relative calm, well at least after the initial chaos and danger.
If we survive and return to Mother Russia let us agree that we will keep in touch and perhaps dine together on occasions but most of all let us agree that at some future date, not too distant, we shall return to Germany and order beer and a meal in this establishment. I do add a footnote here. If this inn has ceased to be an inn then we will find a suitable place nearby."
Chaban looked at the man seated at his desk.
"You see, this is why you have become a most dear friend. What a wonderful, practical idea. It will give us both something to look forward to in the tiresome days ahead. A goal, a little gem to hold onto for the future. I most wholeheartedly agree to your proposal and I insist, no matter whether I am poor and you are rich, that I will pay for the trip, our beds and our food."

A knock on the door interrupted their planning. After a polite hesitation, Hauke Kluge entered. He carried a tray with three

cups and a number of large cakes and buns. He looked quite young. With new clothes and boots procured by his friend Kozuck and his hair a little shorter following an enforced trimming by one of the cooks in an idle moment.
It was his standard procedure to offer to take refreshments to the office knowing that he would be included in the food and drink on offer.

This time there was a degree of silence as he quietly placed the tray on the desk and looked expectantly at the two men. He stepped back. They continued to look at him. Though he did not notice, their faces had reddened slightly.
Of course, something had to be done about the boy. With the changed situation, it was probably time for arrangements to be made for him. While Kozuch could keep him on it would not be fair. There would be little time for him in the new situation. As the man now in charge Kozuch would need to be involved at all times with the management of this sector. The boy would be idle. Lost and vulnerable. Also, the boy needed to be back amongst his own people. He was not a war trophy. It was something that must be done.
Hauke became alert. He looked from one Russian to the other his demeanour suddenly wary.
"What is wrong?" he asked. "Something is wrong."
"Hauke," said Kozuch quietly, "Please sit down. Have some coffee and cake. We need to talk to you."
The boy looked shocked. Like a trapped animal he scanned the room and the men, trying to confirm that all was not well in his small world. His breathing increased. Then he said the words that both men would remember throughout their lives.

"You're not going to leave me, are you? Please, tell me that."
He put his hands to each side of his head and murmured.
"Not again, Not again."

Chapter 10

'Wolfskinder'

"Wolf children? It's not a term I'm familiar with Madam."
The lady looked at the Russians. She was intrigued that two
officers would call at her establishment. Also rather nervous.
"It's a term we have adopted. Little Germans. There are so
many. They have lost everything. We do the best we can to
find a parent or relative but in many cases, there is nobody
to find."
She looked again at the immensely sad boy standing beside
the two men. His head was bowed, there were tears in his
eyes. He held a suitcase and had an army rucksack slung on
his shoulder.
"Of course we can take him. We will find room somewhere.
This is an old convalescence home. By some miracle, it survived the bombing. Even the beds were still intact. He may
have to make do with some blankets on the floor for a while
but we cannot turn any wolfskinder away."

She put her hand to Hauke's chin and lifted his head up so
that he looked her in the eyes.

"I am Frau Gaertner. I will be here for you at all times.
The people here will look after you and although our accommodation is not splendid it is held together with kindness.
It is spring now Hauke. Our back garden has vegetables, flowers and some songbirds. It is a nice place to sit and to play."

Colonel Chaban looked about the long, dark corridor.

A great deal of stained wood and panelling. Sunlight shone in
from a distant rear door. There were faint sounds of activity
from the back and above, up a sizeable curved staircase.

The whole place was constructed of dark ornate timber in a
very German style. It was not cheerful in its aspect but Frau
Gaertner seemed quite sincere in her reassurances of all
good things within the walls.

A boy and two girls descended the staircase. They seemed
about eight years of age. They were barefoot. After a glance
at the Russians, they began to run along the corridor.

"Walking, please," called Frau Gaertner.

They obeyed and made there way out the sunlit door to what
must have been the rear garden.

"It is very kind of you to have taken care of young Hauke for
a period," the lady said. "I'm sure it is not in your normal list
of duties."

Kozuch put his hand on Hauke's shoulder then round his
shoulder to pull him tight.

"I can assure you, Frau Gaertner, this young man has been a
pleasure to have with us at all times."

"Even though he is German?"

"The war is over. He was just a boy who needed a place to
live. And he was most helpful and cheerful to have around.

If circumstances were different we would continue to care
for him but as explained we have both been reassigned so
......"
Kozuch ran out of words. He realised how fond he was of the
boy they were now deserting. None of the real reasons for
Hauke's presence in the sector's Russian administration area
had been divulged. Following the failure to find and capture
the rocket scientist Antek Beck they had located a few of the
scientists working on nuclear fusion projects within Berlin
and had shipped them and their equipment back to Moscow.
It was some compensation. They were not sure how much.

"Well," said Frau Gaertner, "As the officer in charge of this
sector, could you come to my office to give me some more
details and sign some papers."
Kozuch followed the woman through a door past the stairs
leaving Chaban and Hauke alone in the corridor.
"Let's sit down Hauke."
He guided the boy to a bench seat at the base of the stairs.
Hauke sat with his head down then steadily began to cry.
His shoulders shook as he sobbed. It seemed he had been
crying for days.
Colonel Chaban, a senior officer in the Imperial Russian
Army found his own eyes were becoming moist. Angry at
himself he grabbed the boy's hand and dragged him to his
feet. He pulled him round in front of himself and took the
boy's head in his hands, holding his gaze. Staring straight at
the miserable countenance he said with all the passion he
could muster.
"I say this to you, Hauke Kluge. My promotion and move to
our administrative headquarters could be the best chance

you have of finding your beloved Adriane and Dieter. I will
be in a place where all information arrives, where news and
reports are made and where with some careful questions
to certain people in the right places information previously
unobtainable may be procured.
I offer no guarantees my little friend but I swear to you I will
do my very best to find the whereabouts of Adriane and Dieter and pass the information onto you. Do you believe I will
do that for you?"
He let go of the boy's head. Had he been squeezing too tight?
Hauke's gaze did not drop. He continued looking with those
odd piercing eyes of his at this big Russian enemy-man then
he held up his arms. Chabin bent forward to the boy's level.
Hauke put his arms round the man's neck and holding on
tight with his head against the man's cheek, he whispered,
"Yes, I believe you."

Frau Gaertner was a lady of her word. Life as a wolfskinder
was very basic but fair. She had left out the degree of strict-
ness that permeated the orphanage but there was an underlying kindness as well. After two weeks huddled on blankets
in a corner Hauke was granted the bed of a young girl who
was taken into care by a distant aunt.
Nearly all the children were younger than Hauke so he was
expected to show leadership and responsibility.
Frau Gaertner spent a great deal of her time seeking help for
her establishment. Because she had started the whole place
by herself it had taken some time to gain any official recognition. Now that it existed within the framework of the local
German facilities the lady turned her attention to obtaining

extra rations, blankets, beds, pillows, clothing, staff, medical assistance. Her list of wants and needs was extensive and she became somewhat annoying to the people she pursued. Her efforts did pay dividends. Some new sets of gardening tools arrived one day. A doctor was assigned to pay weekly visits.

A permanent, though limited supply of bread was arranged via a local bakery.

Best of all an elderly gentleman arrived one morning and took over all the office paperwork including the ongoing search and follow up of possible relatives and adoptive adults for the children.

He revealed he was eighty years old. He was a former clerk in a Krupps manufacturing plant. His name was Max.

The only other boy of Hauke's age in the building was a fat lazy lad who was somewhat dull and not very good company. Hauke found himself chatting more with Max. Soon he was running messages and sorting files in the office.

Max was stuffy, grumpy and fussy but he was close to the information that Hauke craved. Some hints were issued that would help him find his adopted family. Two people who thought he was dead.

Max was aware of Hauke's case but gave the impression it was beyond him to find anything new that might help.

The months of summer slide over the city. Frau Gaertner organised a sort of pond in the yard. By coaxing the children in for a swim and splash she and her staff managed to get them washed with minimal fuss and at a great saving in time and valuable soap. The whole operation was run with ingenuity making up for the many missing essentials needed for day to day existence.

Alone at times under a garden tree, Hauke would find that he was suddenly overcome with despair and misery. It would come upon him without warning. A sort of hopelessness where he could see no future in his quest to find Adriane and Dieter. What was to become of him? Some children were adopted by families who wanted children or who had lost children but that was only those orphans who had a definite history of all their family being deceased. Also, adoptive families wanted young children, not those who were approaching puberty with all its potential for disruption.
Besides, Hauke wanted to be with Adriane and Dieter not some strangers who may not be kind or understanding. With the war just completed and most systems barely functioning Hauke was just a number in many numbers.

He had not seen the two Russian officers since their tearful parting on the day he arrived. He had hoped that Kozuch would at least visit as he was close by but days turned into other days and they turned into weeks and nothing changed.

It was after one particularly bad bout of melancholia under the garden tree that Hauke wandered across the grass to the building's rear door with a vague notion that he might visit Max to see if there was any small task the man might set him so as to take his mind off his situation.
As his eyes adjusted to the gloom inside he thought he saw Comrade Kozuch follow Frau Gaertner into the building office. It was a momentary thing and as he stood looking along

the big empty expanse of stained timber and worn floor-
boards he decided he must have been mistaken. Then again
it had seemed quite real.
Could he go to the office and walk in as if just seeking some
work to do? It did not seem unreasonable. He lingered for
some time in the corridor unsure of why or what might be
transpiring if in fact Comrade Kozuch was indeed in the office. Surely he would have come to say hello Why would he
be talking to Max and Frau Gaertner?

He was almost at the office door, sidling slowly along the wall
when the door opened and Kozuch stood there.
He was saying over his shoulder, "You say he's in the garden.
I'll go now and find him."
He turned and looked across to where Hauke stood against
the wall, looking slightly embarrassed at being caught loiter-
ing.
"I thought I saw you," he offered.
"Well you did," said Kozuch. "Can we go to the garden? Frau
Gaertner agreed to let me tell you of the developments."
"Is it good news?"
"Well, it is a lot more than I'd hoped for but the puzzle is not
complete."
They reached the garden tree and found two sturdy iron
chairs on which to sit.
Kozuch turned his chair so that he was facing the boy and
their knees were touching. He held up some papers.
"Colonel Chaban has kept his promise. He made extensive
inquiries regarding the whereabouts of your two companions. There are parts of what I know that cannot be divulged
because of your two friends and their connection, even acci-

dentally, to that German man we were seeking."

"Herr Beck?"

"Yes, that man."

"Are they nearby?"

"No," said Kozuch, "but we know roughly where they went. Let me put it this way, we have a good idea of their whereabouts but only an area."

"Why?"

"You must understand Hauke, there are many thousands of displaced people all over Europe at the moment. It is luck in a way that your Adriane and Dieter stood out a little from the crowd. Anyway, Colonel Chaban was able to speak to some of our American allies. At first, they were reluctant to talk because of their own interests in Herr Beck. I am not sure what Colonel Chaban said to the Americans but he somehow convinced them that this was simply a missing person's case and it did not have any 'implications'. It was difficult. He seemed to have lost the last chance. Then he received a call from an American officer."

"And he knew?" Hauke was impatient.

Kozuch put his hands on the boy's shoulders.

"The Americans are willing for you to be transferred to an orphanage in their zone. They say they will then do what they can to seek your friends. They offer no guarantees. They only say that Adriane and Dieter were processed in their zone."

"They made it," muttered Hauke.

"Pardon?"

"So how big is this area, where they might be?"

"The state of Hessen."

Colonel Chaban had also discovered that the Americans had Antek Beck and he was, together with his family already in the United States.

The British were in possession of most of the German atomic scientists.

All the Russians had for their searching was some lesser atomic scientists and the Kaiser Wilhelm Institute of Physics in Berlin. This entire facility was dismantled together with its supplies of uranium and shipped back to Moscow. Generally, they felt cheated.

Chapter 11

'Hessen'

He was to travel alone. There were papers which he had to
present when he arrived at Kassell. All aspects of his sudden
removal to a different part of Germany happened within a
week. Hauke Kluge was a Berlin boy. His whole twelve years
had been spent in this city. Except for trips to nearby lakes
for holidays with his mother, father and brother he knew
little of the rest of his country. A country now in ruins, ruled
by others, exhausted and barely functioning. He was scared
but the thought of moving closer to Adriane and Dieter gave
him hope and courage. Though Comrade Kozuch had reminded him that they would not be looking for him as they
thought he was dead.
"It is all up to you Hauke," he explained. "You and perhaps
some friendly people who may know something or a clerk
in an office for displaced persons who may have a record.
Perhaps an American who can recall your friends passing

through. Most of all some luck. That is what I wish you my young friend, lots of luck. I will always remember you as a fine young person whom I met and befriended once. In a time of conflict, you gave me some optimism. That the world may right itself once more. One final thing. Please take note. Luck is often something you create rather than find."
Hauke looked at the Russian as he thought about the advice.
"I'll use that advice," he said at last. "I will not forget you either. Even as I become an old man."
Kozuch laughed.
"In a way, you're already wise beyond your years."

Max escorted him to the station.
He whispered as they waited on the platform, "This could be a very fortunate move for you boy. Make sure you behave yourself and do not bring further shame upon the German nation."
It seemed an onerous task but Hauke nodded in agreement. The old man must have been a proud German once, before the war.
A train backed into the platform. Black and belching thick smoke. The carriages were damaged with some missing glass and even a couple of rows of holes from strafing but they were functional. Russian soldiers had the first six to themselves with two at the rear for German civilians.
The guard announced that the train would depart in 4 minutes.
"You should board and take a seat," announced Max. "I'll assist with your suitcase."
Hauke glanced along the platform. The Russian soldiers' giv-

en priority were already settling in their carriages. The few Germans taking the trip now climbed into the rear carriages. The platform was empty. The guard was fetching a flag to announce the departure. Time ticked.

A railway official almost skidded as he ran onto the platform at the far end.

"Halt," he called. Halt den zug. Halt den zug."

The guard waited. A few heads appeared from the German carriages. Max had Hauke at the carriage steps.

"Russische Offiziere möchten mit einem Ihrer Passagiere sprechen."

"Is it serious?" asked the guard.

"Nein. Es ist nicht ernst."

Round the entry at the end of the station came Colonel Chaban and Senior Lieutenant Kozuch, walking briskly.

On the train, the fellow passengers had parted and allowed Hauke a seat to himself. This German boy with his blonde hair and odd eyes who was spoken to on the platform and hugged by two senior Russian officers. Their abhorrence of the Russian conquerors was mixed with a great deal of curiosity about the incident.

They watched him carefully throughout the trip.

The journey was slow with numerous stops. Near the end of the Russian zone, the train halted. Hauke was eating some sausage, cheese and bread. A small meal handed to him at the orphanage door by Frau Gaertner as she patted his head and wished him good fortune.

There were heavy footsteps. Hauke leaned out of his seat

and looked along the carriage. He was the only person left on board. A Russian junior officer was checking the carriage seats. When he reached Hauke he looked down with a slight smile and said, "Do you have papers? Why are you still on the train? I do not think you should be here."

Hauke took out the envelope he was told to present to the person on the platform in Kassell.

The Russian peered at all the papers as if seeking some form of trickery. The first few pages were in Russian, German and English. He read them carefully, looked at the other pages in German, looked again at Hauke then curtly handed them back.

"Stay on the train'" he said.

There were Russian soldiers about. Those who had embarked from Berlin had left the train earlier. These soldiers seemed more alert, more organised.

Finally, after twenty minutes the train gave a lurch and moved off.

As they rolled through the Hessen countryside Hauke saw his first Americans. Their trucks and some tanks were parked in compounds.

They seemed more relaxed, sitting about and talking, not as tense as the Russians. He reminded himself that the Americans too had conquered his homeland.

"Are you Hauke Kluge?"

The man on the platform was a short, neat fellow in a crumpled suit. He didn't smile but had the look of somebody who would if he deemed it necessary.

The boy nodded. He was the only person to alight from the

train except for guard and driver. The train then moved on further south with its empty carriages.

"Do you have some papers for me?"

He examined the papers carefully. Nodded a few times then said, "Ah."

Extending his hand he said, "My name is Karl. I will take you to our home for displaced children. You will be fed and cared for while we establish if you can be relocated. Do not hold your hopes high. There are many people who are lost or cannot be found or are dead. We do our best but your stay may be quite long."

Karl picked up Hauke's suitcase. As they walked to the station exit he added, "It seems the Americans may be able to help in your case. I am not sure how or why but we can inquire."

Chapter 12

'Barn Wood'

Dieter looked at the considerable pile of timber in front
of him. Stacked planks in careful piles. Heavier structural
beams and framing pieces. All in excellent condition.
Klaus put his hand on the younger man's shoulder.
"So what do you think of this. I bought it all in 1938 from a
local mill because they were closing down. Then Germany
decided to have a war with the world. My son was enlisted
and he looked very smart in his uniform. At the time I think
I foolishly felt proud of him. We kissed him goodbye right
there by the gate. Assured as we were that the conflict would
be brief, we agreed with a final handshake, that he would
help me use up all this wood as soon as he returned.
We received one letter from him. I'm not sure where he was.
At that time we were all-conquering. It doesn't occur to you
that soldiers die even when you're winning. Then the notifi-
cation every parent dreads. We have no idea where his body

lies. Poland, Belgium, France?

We were blessed with another boy. It is late for us to be parents but at least we have young Lambert as an heir.

So you see, it was uncertainty and fear that made me wait. I've kept it all covered and protected waiting for when the time was right. As I say, Dieter, you help me with my shed repairs then you get the timber you need to repair your barn. It is a good deal for you."

Dieter was about to reply with a remark about getting a strong, fit man to do all the lifting. Then he stopped, realising that he would be replacing the son who failed to return.

"You're right Klaus," he said, "that's a good deal."

Klaus brightened upon hearing this.

"When can you start?" He raised his eyebrows in anticipation.

Klaus had extensive orchards and sheds in which to store his apples and other fruit. Some walls were rotten. In theory, they would not take long to repair.

"I can start tomorrow, Klaus. Is that soon enough?"

They walked together back to the house for morning coffee. Despite his good cheer, Klaus was like many in the district, a rather lost soul with family members gone and old age approaching. Their futures were an unknown land where time was against them.

He was quite a tall man with the air of a bank clerk rather than an orchardist. His line was that he'd decided on growing fruit trees becasue he could pick half the fruit without the need of a ladder.

As they passed one of the storage buildings a young girl in

an apron came out into the sunlight. She had her hair hang-
ing in a single rough plait down past her shoulders. A little
blue bow hung from the end. Her brown eyes flicked up at
the two men.
"Oh," she said, "Hullo Mr Falke."
Dieter smiled. The girl was about twelve and quite pretty.
Slim with a fresh look of youth and bright cheeks.
"Please, there's no need to be so formal Mila, call me Dieter.
We're neighbours after all."
Mila smiled back, shading her eyes from the sun.
"I'll try Mr Falke, oop sorry Mr Dieter."
They all laughed. The girl with her hand to her mouth.

As they continued on Dieter commented.
"Your daughter is a lovely young lady, Klaus."
The man stopped and turned. He looked away.
"Oh, I thought you knew Dieter. Mila is not my daughter.
Though this is now her home and always will be. And she
is loved. A dear friend to young Lambert as well. She is my
sister's child. They lived in Stuttgart. The British bombers
hit their house directly. All inside were killed. "
"Mila?"
"She was playing at a friend's house. She knew nothing till
she walked home and found crowds gathered in her street.
They thought she too was buried in the rubble of her home.
Naturally, we took her in. She is a delight, strong of will and
nature. It took two years before she laughed again. I suspect
she still dreams of a family gone forever. She has seen and
knows too much for somebody so young. Simply sorting fruit
keeps her occupied. There is therapy in handling produce
you know. You will find this yourself as you develop as a

farmer and provider of items to the markets."

At lunch that day Dieter told Adriane of his news. First the arrangements with Klaus regarding swapping his labour for the timber to repair their barn then of the young girl Mila and her circumstances.
They sat in silence for a while. The house was quiet.
It creaked occasionally as clouds passed overhead briefly cutting off the sunlight.
Finally, Adriane spoke.
"So much sadness. So many ruined lives. I consider us so lucky yet you have nobody, I have nobody, that girl has nobody. Where does it end?"
Dieter stood and moved round the table to his wife.
He hugged her shoulders.
"I think it has ended. It seems that all the remaining broken pieces must somehow form a whole again by living and growing and continuing. It is all we can do."
He patted his wife's abdomen.
"Soon a new life will arrive. Our baby will know nothing of what has gone before. The first of the next generation. A new generation who will build all over again. It will take a long time to repair this land but a start must be made."
He kissed the top of his wife's head.
"You know, when we found that room."
"That Magic Room," she corrected.
"Yes, Hauke's Magic Room. I feel it was meant to be. I'm not a believer in a God so let's call it destiny but somehow the pieces were shuffled so that we met."
"All three of us," said Adriane.
Dieter looked out their window to the yard.

"I know. I know. Nothing will bring him back dear wife and wishing will not make it so."

Dieter met Klaus early the following morning. They began stripping pieces of timber from the side of the first building. Naturally, the work was greater than anticipated. Some of the third shed exposed most to the weather had decay damage in the frames. They would need to be replaced before recladding could begin.
Klaus was amused.
"It's the chance you took when agreeing. Besides all of Germany has been endlessly disappointed of late. It's just another slight drawback."
Dieter looked at his neighbour.
"Were you called up to the Volkssturm at the end?" he asked.
"No, we had an enlightened local commander who realised the war was lost. Forming a militia of old men armed with ancient rifles and pitchforks to take on the forces of the United States Army and Air Force seemed to him like a very quick way to kill off what people remained alive in this area of Hesse. It was a brave move on his part. Such acts were called treason and hangings took place. So we tended to our farms and shops and waited while our commander found ways to delay any need to asemble. Unlike those poor bastards in Berlin facing annihilation by the Russians."
Klaus stopped wrenching boards with his crowbar.
"When are you going to tell all of your story my friend? I've heard it from Egon but there seems to be many holes in the fabric. It is thin on details. What have you left out? Does it embarrass you? You are among friends you know. The Germany of secrets is no more."

Dieter stood back. He shook his head.

"I'm sorry Klaus. It's not that I don't want to tell you. Adriane and I gave certain undertakings regarding the arrangements made for us in exchange for our help. It included saying nothing about it."

"You betrayed your country and you're ashamed?"

"No, certainly not. In fact, I think long-term I may have done everyone a favour. Partly from ignorance, partly from a need to survive.

I can say this much Klaus, nobody was harmed or tortured or injured or treated badly by our actions."

"You worked with the Americans?"

"You know I did."

"Well," said Klaus, rubbing his nose, "I will ask no more. The Americans seem quite acceptable as conquerors, so far. Whatever you did with them or for them it must have been of great value. They arranged a house and farm for you after all. If it was something that makes for a better world in the future then that is good."

For a week and then three more days Dieter worked with Klaus to repair and paint his sheds. Mila joined them and was held aloft standing on the men's shoulders to paint the highest planks.

"It's quicker than moving a ladder," they told her.

The only colour available in sufficient quantities for the painting was a rust-red colour, acquired by a local shop whose owner did his best to find supplies. The labels were American though not from their armed forces.

"We're becoming American," said Klaus, viewing the finished work. "Isn't this the colour you see on their farm buildings?"

He leant down with a rag and wiped a drip of the paint from
Mila's nose.

"It may be but they look quite handsome," answered Dieter.

"All the same, I suspect that they are supplying our stores
with such paint so as to turn us American. Propaganda by
stealth. What do you think?"

"I think it's a theory with many possibilities that can be pursued in more leisurely times."

Klaus laughed.

"Okay, beer and pretzels to celebrate the completion of the
work. My gratitude will extend to helping deliver the wood
for your barn."

Chapter 13

'Misplaced'

The food was wholesome and the harried staff did their best. The children were expected to work in the kitchen and the laundry as well as performing cleaning duties and taking care of the smaller ones.
There were similarities to the orphanage in Berlin except for the extensive grounds.
Every few days Hauke would seek out Karl and ask if there was any progress in his case. Karl would look at him with the eyes of a troubled man and say, "No, not yet."

Months passed and soon Karl would avoid the boy rather than face his forlorn, desperate look and his disappointment. The case of Hauke Kluge was complex and Karl found dealing with the Americans difficult because he had very limited English and an interpreter was not always available.
There were more rewarding cases that simply involved

checking lists and connecting names and dates. Many of the children were reunited with parents or a single parent or a relative and could be taken or sent off to resume some sort of stable life.

He was a good boy. He did his assigned work without delay or complaint and was quite popular with the younger children because of his quiet manner and kindness. He had seen this manner in some children. Despite their youth, they had seen and heard too much. Their world was a dark and hopeless place. They became automatons.

When they were given time to play Karl would glance out of his office window and see Hauke sitting alone or standing at the fence staring out across the fields. He would bow his head and turn away promising to look at Hauke's case very soon.

Their home for displaced or misplaced children was located in a Wehrmacht storage facility. The buildings once cleaned out and fitted with beds were quite suitable for their new purpose.

It even had a stout, high wire fence to discourage the little ones from wandering off.

On one such day, Karl observed Hauke once again wandering along the edge of the perimeter fence. Another boy about his age came up to him to talk but after a limited exchange soon walked away. Karl could only guess that Hauke was not ideal company.

He turned away from his window.

"If you don't ring the Americans I will do it myself."

Standing behind Karl was Nurse Meyer. A stout lady with a kind disposition, she came to their facility most days to tend to the children's needs. Now she stood in his way.

"I did not hear you come in Frau Meyer."

"Well?"

"It will lead nowhere. The Russians sent him here just to be rid of him."

"But the Americans said they would help. They would not say that about an individual case unless they possessed some knowledge that may help."

Karl looked sheepishly at the woman standing with her arms folded.

"It was all a conversation between the Russians and the Americans. I was not privy to the details."

"Then contact the Americans and ask."

"They are so difficult to deal with. I have to try to speak English. It gets me nowhere. They're so .... self-assured."

Nurse Meyer became agitated.

"We were at war with them. Yet, now they give us food and medicine. They gave us our beds. They restored working services. Yet you complain about difficulties. That boy is miserable. I will telephone the Americans tomorrow from the hospital. We have two doctors who speak English quite well."

Karl called to the departing figure of Nurse Meyer. Her interest in Hauke lasted from the day she had him strip his shirt and sit on a stool while she washed his hair and noticed the scar on his abdomen. His information about its origins could best be described as vague.

"It will lead nowhere. Then he will be even more miserable," called Karl."

"At least he will know," she called back.

Two days later Nurse Meyer entered Karl's office once more.

"It is arranged. An American officer called Yates is coming here tomorrow. He is driving from Bad Hersfeld especially to see you and to talk matters over. I think he is rather senior. That must mean something. Be on your best behaviour and see what can be done. I'm assured he speaks German."

She swept out the door leaving Karl open-mouthed, his pen halfway through a sentence he was writing.

The man looked annoyingly handsome in his fresh American uniform. He carried a leather briefcase.

"Hullo Karl. Okay, wenn ich dich Karl nenne?"

He closed the office door and held out his hand. It was another annoying habit of the Americans to appear so friendly and to use first names.

"Karl shook his hand and said, "Please be seated."

Colonel Yates opened his briefcase and removed a manilla folder.

"I'll get straight to the point, Karl. We were wondering if this boy had turned up. I mean, we hadn't heard from you so we assumed that the whole thing had fallen through. Now you tell me he's here. So, I've come to explain the situation. It's the least I can do. Put simply, despite my initial indications that we might be able to help I was reminded that it is not within my purview to advance this any further."

Karl hesitated then said, "Pardon?"

Colonel Yates leaned forward.

"The people involved in this particular matter are classed as 'confidential'. To put it another way, we can't talk about this case. Any part of it. For any reason. Ever."

Colonel Yates leaned back and smiled weakly.

"Sorry," he said.

Karl cleared his throat.

"Well .... that, that is most disappointing. I think the boy thought he may be able to find these people again."

Colonel Yates nodded. He put his briefcase on the floor.

"Yes, I understand. It is a shame but sometimes these situations can't be avoided. Powers in high places determine things are a certain way and that is the end of the matter. I am told that the people he seeks think he's dead so they will not be searching for him. Perhaps it's all for the best. You know, long term, for the kid."

The American leaned forward again and put his hands on Karl's desk.

"You know Karl, I'd very much like to meet this young fella. I feel if I explain the matter to him. You know as an American then he'll realise it's not going anywhere and he'll settle down and become a model citizen. Could you do that for me."

Karl did not like this American he seemed a little too 'nice' and too 'casual.' Still, he acquiesced.

As Hauke entered the room, Colonel Yates stood to greet him and shook his hand introducing himself before Karl could speak. The American then found the boy a chair next to him and took charge of the whole conversation.

He told the boy in detail that he had no new information that could possibly help find this Dieter and this Adriane and that the case was not able to be progressed. He hoped that Hauke understood that he could not help. His German was excellent. On several occasions, he drew the boy's attention to the manilla folder on the desk and how it contained virtually no information that would be of any assistance. He stabbed it with his finger emphasising that this was closed case and there was nothing more he could do.

He finished by pointing out that many children will be disappointed with their predicament but they must make the most of what information is at hand and what life presented to them and that it was not always possible to get everything we want.

Finally, Karl was able to break into the discussion.
He resented the way this American had totally dominated the meeting with the boy. This was his office after all and it should be he who conducts and leads the proceedings.
Colonel Yates was now standing. He took his manilla folder and placed it back in his briefcase. It all seems rather pointless to Karl. To make such a show of bringing documents to the meeting only to advise that they could not be opened.
"Well thank you for your time Colonel. Although it has been of no help you clearly pointed out to Hauke that his avenue of enquiry is ended. A dead end as it were."
Colonel Yates shook hands with Karl.
"Yep, sorry, that's the way it goes sometimes."
He turned to Hauke. The boy had not said a word since entering the office.
"I'm glad I met you, Hauke. I wanted to say hullo. See you're okay. Now keep in mind what I said. What happens in the future is pretty much up to you buddy. You can take opportunities as they present themselves and life might work out fine. It's up to you."
He took Hauke's hand and held it, staring into the boy's eyes for some seconds then said, "I hope to hear things work out for you. Do you understand?"

Hauke looked at the hand holding his then back at the Colonel.

"Yes, I think I do," he said hesitantly

"Well," said Karl, trying to gain some authority, "I'm sure we will be able to take care of this boy from here on, thank you." He moved round from his desk ushering the American out the door.

"So good of you to come. Goodbye."

Colonel Yates was gone with a wave.

Karl turned to Hauke.

"I'm very sorry. It is as I suspected there was no news of any interest. Let me give your situation some thought over the next few weeks. I'll see if I can find any arrangements that I feel might suit you."

The boy was strangely quiet. Karl had expected more of a reaction. Either sadness and perhaps tears or anger and frustration.

Finally, he said, "Why don't you go to the kitchen and tell them I said you can have some cake and a drink. Sit outside for a while. Some peace will do you good."

He patted the boy's head as he closed the door and gave an extended sigh. Then he returned to his desk and the files.

Outside, sitting in the sunlight with his back against the building Hauke was deep in thought. He had no cake and no drink, only a nagging puzzle in his head. He waited for inspiration.

Colonel Yates while talking to him had watched his face at all times. He especially watched as he thumped his hand on the folder on the desk. The folder had a corner of a piece of paper protruding from the bottom. It hung out just enough to reveal a word written quite heavily in pencil. The word, spelled out in capital letters was 'WILLINGEN'.

Chapter 14

'Willingen'

A man with dirty hands and rolled up shirtsleeves pulled his little cart to a halt. His small horse began browsing about on the roadside selecting the choicest grass to consume.
The cart was loaded with cabbages.
He turned to the boy sitting next to him on the seat board.
"Well, there you are. It's not too far, past these woods, for somebody young and determined."
He was pointing to a sign that indicated the road to the right. The sign said 'Willingen.'
"If I owned a motorised vehicle I would take you to the town but my little horse is not up to doing side trips. Would you like another drink before you start your walk?"
Hauke stood beside the cart drinking cool water from the man's jug. He replaced the cork and handed it back.
"Thank you."
"It's a warm day," said the farmer, "Aren't you hot in that

coat?"

The boy shrugged.

"Yes, I am but with this suitcase it's easier to wear the coat."

"It's an army coat. You're too young to have been in the army."

"Not in Berlin. It made no difference."

"Oh," said the man. He seemed a little lost for words.

"Well, I must be off. I wish you well young soldier. You'll soon be home again in Willingen. Safe trip."

Hauke Kluge found himself alone at the side of the road. He stared at the sign to a town he had not heard of and a place that may reveal nothing.

For over a month his planning had taken place. By various means, he collected information about Willingen. He stole a map of Hesse from Karl's office. The town was not so far away that he could not reach it. He considered telling Karl or Nurse Meyer but in the end, decided they would not understand and then he would be trapped.

The American officer had said it was all up to him.

The more he thought about that meeting the more convinced he became that the man was giving him a message.

There was a danger he would be missed and quickly found. He would leave at night and hide in forests. He saved a little food and hid it under his pillow but a few days later he found it had gone. No doubt eaten by some of the other inmates. There was a part of the boundary fence at a far corner where the ground sloped sharply downwards. The builders of the fence must have decided that the slope was enough for security. The wire was simply laid against the slope with no support poles. It could be easily lifted.

"Where are you going, young man?"
On his first day after walking all night and hiding in a stand of pine trees for most of the day Hauke had emerged and almost immediately a black car had slid to a halt next to him on the road. The man calling from his car window was smiling with his eyebrows raised. He did not seem the type who would be out hunting for a missing boy. Also, he had a very odd accent.
After considering the situation for a moment Hauke randomly chose a destination.
The man said, "Ah yes, that's on my way."
Hauke climbed in next to the driver on the front seat.
He cradled his case and coat.

The man was a British Army attache. He said he'd been to see the Americans and then he talked about liking to help the young people he saw.
"It was not you who started this terrible war," he espoused.
Hauke had lied about his destination just in case. He told the man he was returning home after staying with his uncle in Kassel.
He chose a town called Ippinghausen as his destination.
A name he remembered from his map.
"How were you planning to get home this day?" the man asked.
Hauke put on his most pleasant smile.
"I hope for friendly people to help me," he replied. "This is my second trip to my uncle and back in weeks."
The man laughed and said it was his pleasure to have

helped.

"You know," he said, "the adults of your country have done the most appalling things. Too horrible for you to imagine. It will take the world a very long time to forgive Germany. However, I cannot apportion any of that guilt or blame to the children. You were just born. It is a sad world you have entered, young man. Very sad."

Near Ippinghausen the man turned off after leaving Hauke at a closed gate which the boy said led to his farm.

Elated at having escaped the city of Kassel, Hauke was now alone on an empty road and it would soon be night.

He walked all night, avoiding the town and finally settling in a pine forest west of the last houses at some late hour. Although the warmer weather was about he shook with the cold after some fitful sleep.

Once it was light enough to see he moved on through the forest. It was not large and there where men at one point cutting trees. They gave him some water. In his planning Hauke had put aside a little food but had not considered a container for some water.

"Where are you headed," they asked.

Hauke decided to take another chance.

"My uncle lives in Willingen. I'm to stay with him."

They looked sceptical.

"That's quite a walk. Whatever your mission, listen, keep a lookout for the police. They're 'helping' refugees to get to their destinations. If they pick up a young one like you it may be that you won't get to Willingen."

Hauke thanked them and moved off.

"Good luck anyway," one of them called.

"They didn't believe me," he thought.

There were a few other people on the roads. Some looked quite down at heel. Vehicles were few. Each time one approached Hauke would move out of sight. Nobody seemed to bother him. He walked all day with a grim determination. He sweated in his heavy coat. His small suitcase became leaden and his walking became automatic. Late in the day his legs ached and cried a little at the pain. His boots hurt but there was no dark forest to enter and rest. As night fell he found a hollow next to a tree in a field. Several cows watched him suspiciously. It was damp but afforded protection from sight. He ate his last piece of dry bread, hard to swallow with no water.
Curled under his coat he sighed in quiet misery and fell asleep.

When he woke the sun was up. He was chilled and his coat was damp from dew. He licked the coat surface and dabbed his dry lips.
Sitting up looking about he could see a road sign in the distance. Most German road signs had yet to be replaced after their removal by the retreating armies of the Reich in an attempt to confuse and slow the enemy forces rolling across Germany.
When he approached this one it looked home-made. It said Korbach. He consulted his map running his finger across from Kassel. A smile spread on his sore lips. He had covered a much greater distance than he realised.

Leaving the road completely he trudged across a series of

fields to the north of the town then found his way back to a
road that seemed to head west. At the last moment with the
road in sight, some cows trotted towards him and he ran to
the fence. At the fence, they hung over looking at him.
Perhaps they had just wanted some company.

Back on the road feeling slightly elated Hauke found that he
had to stop. His legs were so sore that he could not walk.
He sat at the side of the road on a grass bank, massaging his
calves rocking backward and forwards.
The man was almost upon him before he noticed. An old
farm cart with wooden slab sides.
He pulled gently on the horse's reins. "Halt, halt," he said.
He leaned over with his elbow on the side of the seat.
"Are you going this way? Would you like a ride?"
He was pointing the right way. Hauke stood unsteadily.
He wobbled.
"Yes, yes, I would like a ride. My legs are sore," he said, as he
made his way to the cart.
Once underway before the man could ask his destination,
Hauke inquired, "Do you have any water? I am terribly
thirsty."
"Oh ho," said the farmer, "How patient are you? I have no
water left in my jug but soon there will be a place where we
can both partake of some fine cool water. A little stream with
no name that comes straight from the hills. The water is
delicious."

With his stomach full of water and the man's water jug
topped up they set off once more along the road. The man
had insisted Hauke remove his boots and socks at the

stream and sit for a minute with his legs in the cold water. It had soothed his aching muscles quite well.

An army truck overtook them. It gave a brief tap on its horn to let them know its approach.

"Americans," the man said, as the truck disappeared.

"Now tell me, young fellow, to where are you headed?"

"To Willingen."

"Oh," said the farmer once more. "Well, I can take you to the turnoff. It will give your sore legs more time to rest."

Hauke Kluge was on a road that led to Willingen. He was still struggling. His legs where resenting each step. It was still morning. He could make it by the afternoon he thought. What he would do once he reached the town he was not sure. Buried in the back of his mind was a terrifying possibility that his trip would be in vain and he would find nobody. He despaired at what he would do if this were the case.

He was on the left side of the road passing some forested land when a roar came from behind and a slight screech of brakes.

He looked up startled. Sitting next to him, its motor rumbling away was an American jeep with four big American soldiers on board all looking at him.

"Ich habe dich dort nicht gesehen, kiddo."

The man's German was halting. "Didn't see me? What is a 'kiddo'?"

'Wohin gehst du?"

"I'm going to Willingen," answered Hauke.

The men sat for a moment then looked at each other.

"Naw," said the driver, "No room and besides we're not sup-

posed to pick up any more locals. Let's not upset Sarge."
The front seat passenger looked at Hauke.
"The kid looks ready to drop. How's about we take his case
and his coat. Drop 'em off. That'll help."

It took some minutes for Hauke to understand the offer.
He was concerned that he'd lose his possessions. Equally
the Americans were confused when he said he didn't have
his destination address.
"The Post Office," one of them finally said. "Perfect. They'll
hold his gear an' he can check with dem 'bout where he
wants to go. I mean if they don't know then nobody will
know. Gotta help the little guy. He looks like he needs it."

Hauke watched the jeep roar off with his case and coat
onboard and a wave from the departing soldiers. Apart from
that Colonel, it was his first encounter with American soldiers. He was holding a small bar of chocolate. It said, 'US
Army Field Ration D'. Hauke had not eaten chocolate for
about two years. It tasted wonderful.
After passing fields and some outlying houses, he reached
the town of Willingen by late-afternoon. The Post Office was
an untidy shop in the main street. Hauke Kluge bowed his
head in silent prayer and entered.

Chapter 15

'Homecoming'

Lena Koch was a woman who ran her life, her husband and the post office with efficiency. All three had survived the war by keeping busy and keeping a very low profile. She and her postal assistant husband Hans hated the Nazi Party, the Fuhrer and the terrible things they had done yet she spoke no word of these sentiments to anybody anymore. The consequences of such talk were still raw within her. Lena was a survivor and she accepted what she could not change.

Now late on this warm day of early summer a dishevelled, dirty, sweaty boy had entered her post office and leaned wearily on her counter. He looked pitiful but in her role as postmistress she retained her detachment from matters that were not immediately of concern.
"Are you seeking something?" she asked.
"Did some American soldiers leave my case and coat here?"

She eyed the boy for a second to consider the possibility that he was not the rightful owner when it was obvious it could only be him.

"Yes, they did," she said at last.

She reached down behind the counter and lifted up the case and coat.

"Here. Will there be anything else?" she asked, knowing from the information left by the Americans that the owner of the case and coat might need some assistance in locating a relative or something in the town.

Lena Koch and Hans had never been blessed with children. Well hidden inside her bosom was a fondness for the young. She knew already she would help this boy with his strong eyes and lank hair that may once again appear blonde if enough soap were applied.

"I'm looking for my relatives. Their names are Dieter Falke and Adriane Gerst. They live somewhere in Willingen. Can you give me their location? A street and a number?"

The boy looked pitifully hopeful, his face bright with anticipation. He waited while the woman raised her eyes to the ceiling in thought.

"No," said the postmistress. "I don't know those names." The boy now looked devastated. The woman thought he was close to tears. She put her hand on the boy's clenched fist and added hurriedly, "That does not mean that they are not here. The German postal service is still being rebuilt and there are restrictions. Many people do not send or receive mail. Do you see?"

Then she added somewhat harshly.

"They have no one left to correspond with anymore."

"Oh," said Hauke, "I hadn't thought of that. Do you know

everybody in Willingen?"

"No, I don't know everybody. This is not the town it was before the war. So, your relatives might well be here."

The door to the post office opened and a middle-aged man entered. He was chubby and had red cheeks. Something told Hauke he liked beer.

"Hans," the woman said, "This boy is looking for some relatives with the name of Gerst or Falke. Have you heard of such people?"

"Hmmm, hmmm," uttered Hans closing the door. "No," he said. "This is a time for a list."

Hauke was treated to some hot milk and biscuits in the back of the shop. His first food for a day and a half. He was starting to like these postal people. The lady was nice under her efficient exterior.

Hans had a list of five.

"Descriptions may help," he said, "and age and background." Hauke described Adriane and Dieter with details of what age he thought they might be.

Hans ran his pencil through three of the names.

"Too old. However, I think I have your relatives. There's a couple of people in Zur Hoppecke. It must be them. I've seen them about town. The others are on a farm out of town. Your relatives are city people, not farmers. I'll draw you a map. It's not far. I would take you there but I only have use of the van on Mondays and Fridays and today is Tuesday."

Sometime after Hauke had left them Lena Koch turned to her husband.

"Isn't the man in Zur Hoppecke a former resident of Willingen? I'm sure it was mentioned that he was returned from the war. If so, you may have given false hope to that young fellow. Go see if you can find him.”

The building was small. It had a downstairs parlour that Hauke could see through the window. It looked cosy. He knocked again. This time he heard footsteps descending the stairs. Then the door opened. The man was slim and had quite black hair. He had a small beard.
He just said, “Hullo,” with an inquiring look on his face.
“Do you live here?”
“Yes, I do. Why?”
“I’m looking for my relatives,” Hauke answered, his head down, his voice soft. Already defeated.
“Well, I’m afraid you’ve got the wrong address here.”
The man looked as if he was about to close the door when he said, “What are your relatives names?”
“Adriane Gerst and Dieter Falke.”
“Ah,” said the man, “Dieter. It might be him. Certainly you could try. I’ll get a piece of paper.”

After the boy had gone the man in Zur Hoppecke, Markus Keller, thought it may have been decent to offer him a bed for the night. The farm was quite a long walk but the boy looked as if he could cope. Then he had some doubt. The boy had really looked quite weary.
He walked outside to a few of the side streets in the hope of finding his visitor but there was no sign of him. He did meet Hans Koch also seeking the boy.
“So you gave him my address.”
“If only we had some transport.”
“I have a motorbike,” said Markus..

"Excellent," said Hans.

"Unfortunately it has mechanical problems at the moment."

Hauke followed the road from the town. As the night settled in he realised that he would not make his goal and the man's description and rough map required daylight to help in the search.

Once again he found a few trees on the edge of a field within which to make a camp. He had no food or drink. He lay on his back with his coat over him and looked up through the tree branches to the stars. Dieter was a fairly common name. Nothing was certain. The man had sold this particular Dieter a box of nails in the shop where he worked. To repair a barn, he had been told. A barn that had caught fire from combusting hay. He knew which barn and which farm the man meant. The previous owners had died. They had chatted for a while the man admitting that farming was new to him. It was this last revelation that gave Hauke Kluge hope as he drifted to sleep.

He was awake again as the sun streamed through the trees casting long shadows over the field of some sort of yellow plants. He quickly brushed himself down, miserable with hunger and thirst. His body ached from the cold ground. Making his way back to the fence he climbed over and out onto the road. The hollow in which he'd slept had been very damp. His clothes were wet.

Just as he awoke he heard a vehicle go past toward the town. The road was empty now. It seemed dusty. The sun already had some heat. He began walking, studying the man's notes. After a straight stretch, the road curved and began to rise.

He passed a gate with a note hanging limply.

It said 'Eggs For Sale.'

Hauke was so tired. He felt weak. His legs were already hurting again and he could not ignore his thirst.

He stopped several times and sat on embankments trying to summon power into his small frame.

'At the top of the hill is a covered farm gate with stone walls.' Hauke looked at the words on his note then squinted ahead in the bright light. He thought he could see a high structure a long way off ahead. It was hard to say. He stumbled on up the slope his walk continuing to be painful. Several more times he stopped to rest then took deep breaths and forced himself to continue.

His vision seemed to be blurred. He wanted to fall.

At the top of the hill as he neared the structure his heart became a little lighter. Indeed. A covered gate with stone walls. If nothing else it offered some shade. His mouth was so dry he could not properly feel his tongue.

He consulted the note again blinking hard to focus, checking it for any other words as if he might find some morsel of information he had overlooked. Down the road, further on, no other structure or gate presented itself in the manner of the note's description.

He wanted to go in but the thought of his last option disappearing as he stood before some strangers who did not know him or want him, rose as a choking fear. He was so tired, beaten down and almost finished. He sighed hoping for some sign, some guidance. None came. It must be done.

Walking forward he unhooked the gate and passing through closed the gate once more. His hands shook He then turned and taking up his case and coat began moving forward.

As he made his way slowly along to the farmhouse he noticed for the first time a large barn near the house. He thought there was a man on the roof. His muscles tightened. His steps became agony. He felt faint. The world was washing away and each step became harder. The burden of a life ripped apart was becoming too much for his twelve-year-old frame to carry. His head was now bowed and his walk a shuffle. Hopes, wishes, dreams all hung in the morning air. Hunger, thirst, exhaustion or the prospect of failure were all factors as he tried to progress. He dropped his case and coat.

When he looked up again he was much closer to the house. A woman stood in the yard staring at him. He thought her mouth was open but his eyes played tricks. She was a vague apparition. He blinked repeatedly and squeezed his eyes shaking his head, trying to clear his sight. Sweat ran from his forehead. He took a few more hesitant steps and stopped not able to go on. Lifting his head he looked at the woman. His mouth moved but he couldn't speak, his breath coming in fast pants.

Then she screamed. It was a scream that both startled him and finished him. He sank to his knees. Waited like a prisoner at a beheading for it all to end. Footsteps running.

She was there. Holding him, crushing him with the intensity of a person possessed. She cupped her hands round his face and stared into his eyes. Eyes that saw only a fog. She kissed his cheeks. Frantic in her attention.

It was now that he knew.

He gave in and cried. His body shook as he was caressed and
loved and accepted. It was over.

PART TWO

Chapter 16

'1943

It was a bright morning. The air still held a crisp reminder of the recent winter but only as much as to make an early hot breakfast all that more enjoyable. The newly risen sun cast elongated shadows between the buildings inside the fence. It gave the area a Gothic appearance.

A man, an officer, made his way from the barrack's mess to a set of steps that were in the path of the sunlight. He sat and produced a crumpled Atikah packet from the top pocket of his uniform jacket. Then lighting up one of the cigarettes and peacefully smoking, blowing puffs into the sharp air, spitting out occasional pieces of tobacco.
The quality of the Reich's cigarettes had declined since the war began. He closed his eyes for a moment enjoying the warmth of the new day leaning back on one elbow.
He wore his uniform with an air of self-assuredness. This was his world and he was one of the people who controlled it.

His legs were crossed, his boots shone.

In the distance, down past a series of large brick buildings were some steel gates and a check-point. Across the top of the gates up high for all who entered to see, were some words, spelled out in a wavy pattern of wrought iron. 'Arbeit Macht Frei'.

It always amused the man when he looked that way.

Lower ranked soldiers passed by but they did not bother to salute. It was a relaxed atmosphere. Today would be a good day. The man enjoyed his job. He considered himself quite clever. His abilities in his particular area meant that he was well regarded amongst his peers. There had been no 'disturbances' since he had taken on his role. The 'Charmer' they called him.

The first group was not due for another hour because of a backup in the system. A time to relax and feel the sun and the light breeze. After several days of rain that made sections of the camp muddy and difficult to negotiate, sunshine would render his work a little easier. It was the psychology of the situation.

Despite his uniform and the Totenkopf symbol on his hat, his words, the words, that he had refined to create a perfect balance of 'routine' and 'care', were accepted by the groups as they listened.

New arrivals were the best. They were confused and still carried a little hope in their breasts, that it would all work out okay once the processing was complete. Those who knew the system, those who had spent some time here, they presented a challenge. They were suspicious. Words were spoken even though they should have been avoided.

The truth of the situation was more obvious. Perhaps, in the end, they just accepted the whole business as the way it was to be. Something they could not change or affect and whose outcome was inevitable. It interested this officer that people could have all of their life-force so completely cancelled by circumstance, that they just shuffled to their death as if queuing for a bus or tram.

A soldier presented himself at attention in front of the man on the steps. He did salute.
"Scharführer Meler. I have your list."
He handed over a single sheet of paper.
Meler did not change his position. He returned the salute rather casually and dismissed the man.
The list had only one other entry. Another group this afternoon. In both cases, newly arrived Polish Jews. Though the second lot included Russian Jews.
It would be a quiet day overall.

It was his manner that won them over. Having a stethoscope round his neck was another nice touch but it was the way he spoke and the words he used. Carefully practiced supposed interpreters were on hand to translate his message as well.
It was all theatre.

"I repeat, please remove all your clothing and make sure you fold and place the items together in a neat pile on the benches so that you can easily find them once you return. We apologise for having males and females entering the disinfecting showers together but our limited facilities do not allow for the luxury of separate shower blocks for this

purpose. I'm sure your modesty will survive the encounter. Please bathe yourselves thoroughly and take advantage of the soap supplied. Remember this is a health requirement of this camp and it is in everybody's interest to remain clean and free of germs and lice. It ensures that no outbreaks of fever or disease can occur and cause illness.
Finally, if any of you have any health issues please be sure to mention them to myself or my staff once you are out of the shower block so that suitable medical treatment can be provided. I thank you for your cooperation ladies and gentlemen. We will talk again shortly.
Please proceed."

In most cases, the group would file into the change room with no further interest. More concerned no doubt at having to undress in front of others. His assistants often accompanied the group into the shower room and assisted the frail. The Sonderkommando members also went in chatting about camp gossip and transfers to other work facilities. Always wary of any slip of the tongue which would see them despatched themselves within minutes.
Originally the men and women were handled separately which caused anxiety. It was his initiative to suggest that having mixed groups would be more 'reassuring'.
It was his special touches, the soap, the suggestion of medical help that mostly sent them in without trouble.
Occasionally one would ask why their children were not with them.
"Your children are of particular concern," he would say.
"We take extra care in giving them each a medical examination. So that they are fit for their new life. Children can suc-

cumb very easily to outbreaks of disease. Our work camps will run most effectively when all the workers and their families are healthy and happy. Together once more.
I hope you understand."
They always did.
From the change room with their clothes carefully arranged on the benches, they all made their way, barefoot and huddled, into the giant shower room with rows of shiny chrome overhead water spouts. One or two even dripped. Surely an indication that this was indeed a cleaning facility but actually another clever innovation by Scharführer Meler.
Once inside and quiet the German soldiers and the Sondercommando retreated. The steel door was then quietly closed and locked behind them.

Sealed canisters of Zyklon-B pellets were opened by masked soldiers on the roof. The pellets were immediately introduced through false air vents leading to the chamber below. With the vents sealed once more the pellets were remarkably effective. Apart from a very brief noise as the occupants realised their predicament and sometimes a few seconds of frantic bashing on the door the room very quickly fell silent. It was then a simple matter of awaiting the dispersion of the gas before sending in the Sondercommando to remove the bodies and hose down the room in preparation for the next group.

A man of a similar age to the officer lounging on the steps approached and sat down beside him. He also wore the Schutzstaffel uniform. The rank was also that of a Scharführer.

At a casual glance, these two men could have been related.
Both wore their hair in a similar fashion. Hair that was a light
sandy colour if not blonde. Their eyes were grey-green, not
blue. They were slender but had strong shoulders.
They wore their uniforms with flare and kept them tidy.
Their boots were equally shiny.
There were differences. The one called Meler was shorter.
The new man possessed a sabre cut on his cheek despite the
Reich's dislike of such boorish marks of elitism.
Their demeanour, however, was twin-like.
"How about one of your cigarettes, my friend?"
"Good day, Herr Klein."
Meler handed over his cigarette packet after taking another
for himself.
"I've not seen you for a few days. Have you been busy?"
Scharführer Klein took a deep draw on his cigarette and let
the smoke billow out of his nose. He picked some tobacco
from the tip of his tongue.
"Very much so, Herr Meler. New ideas have been tested.
With great success, I might add."
He flopped down on the stairs next to his contemporary.
Scharführer Klein was involved in the main camp business
but in a semi-research area.
He worked with Oberscharführer Klehr in devising new ways
to efficiently carry out and run the programs.
Their latest efforts were proving satisfactory in treating
certain categories of inmates that may otherwise prove
time-consuming and difficult.
The Klehr method of which he was most proud involved the
use of a long-needled syringe allowing direct injection of
phenol into the heart. This caused a quite rapid cessation of

heart muscle activity and a quick and easy despatch.

Initially, the 'spritzen' technique was employed on peasants and the more 'simple' of the rural male arrivals who did not question the need for lifting their shirts for pseudo-medical people who wished to assess their health. These specimens were generally quite muscular and could have created problems going through the normal system however they readily complied if they thought they were being considered for a job doing farm work.

Being greeted by a man in a white coat who merely wanted to listen to their chest with his stethoscope seemed a harmless exercise. He was seated on a chair with a small stool for the patient opposite.

Once seated the man was requested to lift his left arm up and across his eyes to allow access to the chest area.

At first, the cold but reassuring stethoscope was placed on the chest.

Then the needle was plunged, with some force between the ribs and into the heart, at the same time delivering a lethal amount of phenol.

As long as the whole action was carried out precisely, this method proved an excellent cost-efficient form of despatch. However, there were a few incidents where the recipient became suspicious or was misdelivered the dose thus a violent encounter took place and the guards had to enter the room and shoot or bayonet the disruptive person.

The procedure was still acceptable and continued to have support however it required some thought as to where best it should be used.

The answer was obvious once the various groups were considered.

Scharführer Meler had previously weighed up the benefits
or otherwise of having the children belonging to each group
accompany their parents to the showers. While generally,
the process went satisfactorily, even with those who knew
or suspected the outcome, there was a quite significant time
delay factor as children were settled and coaxed to join in.
The answer was to have the children dealt with via a second
system. One that suited their circumstances.

"It was remarkable," said Klein, leaning back on his elbows
on the wooden steps. He ashed his cigarette to the side.
Pushed his cap back on his head.
"Children think doctors are completely trustworthy.
Never any suspicion. We had over sixty Jews from the last
Polish shipment. They were from four to about twelve in age.
I've got to tell you if you did not know you could have been
mistaken in thinking they were pure Germanic stock. Quite
well proportioned they were. Handsome even. Only their
blood was impure.
A strong resolve was needed to rid us of these creatures and
their false existence.
Oberscharführer Klehr sat in the corner to observe.
He was delighted with our efficiency.
I had two men outside removing their shirts and tops.
They were then ushered in one at a time. I sat behind and
held their arm up while one of the men did the pretend
stethoscope touch. Being small they were so easy to reach
over and position the syringe. Bang. First time every time.
Straight in. A startled sort of jump then they slump and
they're carried out to a room where we had told them there

was hot chocolate drink and biscuits. No noise. Just rapid removal of life. Ridding the world of the Jewish curse. A world that will be so grateful for our work.

By the time we reached halfway, we improved our time by fifty-percent. Not one gave us any trouble. Some of the younger ones smiled.

It is the way of the future, my friend. A complete system. You will not be bothered by children in your showers anymore. All taken away by my brilliance."

Meler laughed.

"Oh, you're so clever. What is your age limit? Will you take older Jews who might fight back?"

Klein shoved his friend's arm.

"Hah, no. Twelve years and down. That's how it works best." He stubbed his cigarette.

"Say, would you like to participate in the next batch? Get you away from just making speeches. That's lazy. This is hands-on involvement. It is quite satisfying."

Meler turned his head to look at his compatriot. He gave a slight smile touching his cheek as if in thought.

"Yes ...... I would like to join in. I can add such knowledge to my file. It might aid in promotion."

Klein leaned to the ear of the man next to him and smiled as would a conspirator.

"Oh, there is more. Often, of late, I've been choosing some of the older ones for a bit of 'enjoyment' beforehand. You will find it most diverting. We get rid of them separately afterwards. There are no rules. I mean no rules. Invention is the name of the game. How clever are you my friend? We will see if you can think of some new sport we can try."

Chapter 17

'1945'

There were perhaps forty Germans in their group.
New days presented new challenges. Assigned menial tasks
such as gardening and cleaning the ladies made sure that
they kept out of sight and out of mind as much as possible.
A new year had just begun but there was no more certainty to their ongoing existence. They saw the never-ending
'groups' brought in and moved on. The lists seemed arbi-
trary except for the obsession with the Jews. It seemed they
were being brought from all over Europe.
Certain officers stood out. The ones to avoid. They relished
their work. Rumours of their methods, their cruelty, their de-
viance, their departure from all morality were passed around
like the Grimms tales told on dark nights.
Each German inmate also had their personal story to tell.
While their circumstances varied, it came down to insulting
or opposing the Third Reich. Something not tolerated in the

new powerful omnipresent Germany.

All were surprised that they had finished up in this place. Extermination camps were for others surely. Many arrived with husbands. Some with families. All were separated and did not know whether the others still lived.

Until they arrived they did not know of nor could they conceive of such places. Purpose-built by fellow Germans for the sole occupation of murdering millions.

Auschwitz was not a town they knew. Stories were told of many other such establishments in other towns and countries. Now they knew of the many terrors this place could hold. Daily existence became an obsession. They stayed away from the arrivals as much as possible. The ones who would be quickly 'moved on'. There was no purpose to it. Being German a conversation with those being processed would be viewed with suspicion. Also, it would always lead to that question. They could not and would not answer. What was to become of them would soon be known.

There was the added fear that some zealous official would decide to make up his numbers and look round for a nearby group.

Today, Lena Koch was watching a work detail being walked to trucks for a task outside the camp. She did this many times but never saw her husband. It was no different this time.

Despite the first bitter hint of winter with a sharp wind blowing between the buildings, it was decided that as there was a little sun shining upon them, they would be tending the gardens near a staff kitchen. Food for officers. They all made a point of furtively spitting on each and every cabbage, onion,

carrot they collected. A pointless but satisfying act to bring
about a feeling of defiance.

While each dawn was approached with caution Lena's group
was full of gossip this day. Their single guard was a low-
ranked SS trooper who seemed disinterested in his job or his
life. His obvious low intelligence or motivation ensured that
his war had lacked any progress since he first gained entry
in the Schutzstaffel. This duty was a particularly embarrass-
ing exercise. Guarding a bunch of German women. What
could they do? Yet he often drew this detail. If he spoke at
all it was to tell them that he was miserable and so they'd
better be careful. His transparent bluff soon vanished and
he settled down somewhere to talk to himself. He had been
known to fall asleep.

There was a change. Everybody noticed it. The officers did
not have the same strut as before. Their walk was often head
down, as if wrestling with a problem. When in groups they
would talk earnestly and gesticulate in a frantic manner.
The bravado was gone. They were distracted, apprehensive,
perhaps more dangerous.
The transports too had slowed. Fewer arrivals but more of
the regulars and those who kept away from the showers by
various means of cunning and subterfuge were now disappearing. None of the group had seen any children for a while.
Activity outside the camp increased. Heavy earthmoving
equipment came and went. A lot of smoke could be seen
in the sky some way off. It was accompanied by a familiar
sweet, sickly smell.
Some said they saw planes flying overhead. They were up

very high. It is possible they were not Luftwaffe.

The weather broke a fortnight later. Snow rushed across the landscape. It coated the bunkhouses and buried the filth and muck on the grounds. Activity initially slowed. The camp seemed to have ceased activity. Officers spent more time in the mess, eating, smoking, talking,
Too far away for any of the discussion to be heard.

In the night a week after the snow started they were huddled together in a range of bunks. Recently the whole bunkhouse was theirs alone.
One of the women sat up. She jolted from the middle of their bodies. Her head was tilted. Her face blank.
"What?" said her companion. "What?"
"Don't you hear it? Listen."
Now they all slowly joined her. Sitting with blankets wrapped round their shoulders.
"There's nothing to hear. Go to sleep," they said, after straining for a minute to hear anything.
"No, no. Take off your scarves. Uncover your ears. Wait."
They waited, their breath forming a white fog in front of their mouths.
Then, they all heard it.
"That's artillery, gunfire. There are explosions. It's fighting. Why can we hear fighting? Who can be fighting so far inside greater Germany."
The sounds died down an hour later. The women eventually returned to their sleep

When morning came they received some extra bread. The

watery soup that constituted their first meal each day and varied from foul-smelling to worse, was thicker and contained recognisable vegetables.

"Did you spit on this," they laughed.

"Stay in your bunkroom till called!" The SS officer was of a higher rank. They had not seen him before. He shouted the same message in the doorway of each building in their compound.

"I don't like this. Called for what?"

"Surely not?"

"They are tidying up. We are in the way."

"Oh God, I knew it would come to this. When a man turns his people against each other like crazed animals ....."

They all sat on the sides of their bunks, shivering partly from cold, partly from fear. There was little point in talking. They knew the possibilities.

A noise at the doorway caught their attention.

"You want this?"

It was their surly guard. He placed a basket of bread and lard on the floor and turned to leave. More food was most unusual. It was a first time.

"What is happening?" Lena called to his back. He turned with his usual disinterested countenance.

"You're leaving. We're all leaving."

"Leaving? Why? Leaving for where?"

"Gross-Rosen I hear."

"Are we waiting for the trucks to take us?"

"Yes, of course. That's it. Your transport is being arranged." The soldier gave a short laugh. It was the only time they heard him laugh. He continued to chuckle and talk to himself as he wandered away.

A few kilometres from the camp on a rise they were able to see part of the immensity of Auschwitz and Birkenau for the first time. Many fires were burning. Some structures were being destroyed with explosives.
"All for killing," said one of their group, "Endless killing. What a terrible place. The world will not forgive them."
"You women. Shutup," a guard cried. "Walk silently or there will be consequences."
They were on a sealed road with banks of snow on either side. Already their feet were cold and they were tired. Pushed together with little space about them.
The guards were angry. Taking turns at walking with them to keep the lines moving. Having short breaks, riding on trucks, before arguing about whose turn it was to get down and walk again.
On the next hill, a quick look behind revealed a massive stream of people trudging in a great grey mass along the road. All heading in the same direction.
"Can they seriously think we can walk all the way?" whispered one of the group.
"I don't think they care." said another. "I have a mind that the war has gone badly. We are retreating."
"Back to Germany?"
"Where else."
" I notice there are no senior officers. Only the Waffen and the foot soldiers."
"Are the rats abandoning the ship?"
"So it would seem."

"Quiet," said a guard.

For a while, they carried on in silence. Occasionally a local
Polish woman or child in a house or farm would pull a window curtain aside just a little, to view the endless bodies
moving past. Their interest would be replaced by fear and
the curtain would be closed once again.
"I am tired. When will we rest? I need to rest. It can't hurt to
sit for a while," said one.
Lena touched her sleeve."
"Don't stop, Whatever. Do not stop."

At 2pm there was a call to halt. The column was on a wide-
open area with fields. A chill wind slid across the ground.
"Sit and rest," yelled two soldiers.
"Sit where?" they muttered. "On the snow and freeze our
extremities?"
Some did sit. One group sat hunched together, trying to de-
feat the breeze.
"Why here, for God's sake? We're exposed on all sides."
"Exactly." said a Jewish woman. They can watch us easily.
No slipping away to freedom and a good life."
There was gentle laughter.
"They don't want us in Germany because we're 'Ekelhafte
Juden'. Yet now, where are we going?"

The army trucks were driven off the road. Hanging from the
back of each protected by the roof and tarpaulin flaps sat
two soldiers, rifles ready, watching the column.
"The bastards are in there eating."
"Hot food, while we starve."

"Nothing has changed. Just their methods."

By night they were stopped in a forest. Told to lay down and stay still. Exhaustion would keep them from moving.
As the light had faded there were rifle shots. Sporadic cracks of a soldier's gun. It was not necessary to discuss the reason. The trucks patrolled up and down the road through the night. Some were run over, sleeping too close to the road.

At the first hint of morning light, they were told to rise and begin moving. As the women stumbled back onto the road they noted that some of the Jews had not risen. They were bayoneted by the guards. Possibly for no good reason.
One of their group became bold. As a guard walked past she asked a question.
"When will we eat?"
The soldier was old and stocky in build. He looked weary. It could have meant that he was a long way past tolerant. He stopped, turned and looked at the woman. He raised his rifle but it suggested more of an automatic response than any menace.
"At the destination," he said. "Get moving."

In the late part of the morning, their road became muddy. It wound uphill through pine trees. Heavy snow was piled on the trees and at their bases. On one side the land sloped away buried in snow. On the other, there was a vertical cut-away embankment of two metres.
The crack of rifle shots became more prevalent. They passed some with black holes in their foreheads and the bright red stain behind.

The guards were not as active running up and down the column. Their dislike of the mud kept them close to the trucks.

Lena Koch ceased mentally to be part of her group. Her mind was focused on each step as though every placement of her foot needed her complete concentration. If she did not continue to give all of her being to her onward motion she knew her legs would cease to obey and the inevitability of such a lack of action scared her into the ongoing effort.

When a hand was placed on her shoulder her mind raced between annoyance that somebody would interrupt her struggle and the possibility that this was the guard who felt it was time to end her journey.
She half-turned her head squinting at the person beside her. Her eyes were watering. It was hard to see. It was a man.
"Hans," she whispered, considering delirium.
"Keep walking," the man said. "Don't look at me."
She cleared her throat. At first unable to speak.
"Is it really you? Please say it is."
"Yes, it's me."
"You're alive."
"Apparently so."
"How ...... "
"Destiny, a miracle, who knows. The same with you?"
"I suppose."
"I saw you yesterday as they walked us out of the gates.
I was overjoyed. They held us back and you were marched off. I have been slowly and very carefully making my way through the column to reach you."
Lena stumbled. She gave a little cry.

"Put your hand on my arm. Don't make it obvious."

After Hans Koch had glanced about to ensure there were no guards nearby he spoke again.

"Listen, I want the two of us to slowly drop back into the midst of these Jews behind us. The poor devils are so weak the guards are not bothering to watch them. They just shoot them when they drop. We must get to the middle of them and near the edge."

Hans Koch checked about once more, lifting his head a little and surveying their immediate position.

Again he spoke.

"We can't go on like this. Over this hill in a few minutes the snowbanks at the side will be much deeper. I have a plan. Are you with me, dear wife?"

Lena looked at her husband.

"I remember our vows," she said, trying to smile with her cracked lips.

Chapter 18

'Now Three'

Adriane was possessed, by love, a need to care and guilt.
From the moment they lay him on a bed, bathed his face
and then let him fall into exhausted sleep she had no other
purpose but to tend to this miracle boy who had reappeared
in their lives.
Once awake some eleven hours later, in the middle of the
night, she made him hot soup and bread, bacon and potatoes and tea. She sat with him as he ate continually touching
his hands and face as if confirming his existence.
They talked and Dieter joined them. His story was long and
complex. He pulled up his shirt and showed them his scar.
The Russians, the hospital, Captain Chabin and Comrade
Kozuch.
"I'm sorry but they were nice to me. Like two Uncles. I am
here because they started my journey for me."
He told of the Berlin orphanage, the second orphanage, the

nice American Colonel Yates.

They stopped him there and began to tell their story of their escape from Berlin, their friend Rolf who helped them to the border and of their meeting with the Americans and with Corporal Yates.

"Yes," they said, "He was most certainly trying to help you."

"You call him Corporal?" said Hauke. "I'm sure he was a Colonel. Is that better?"

Dieter looked from Hauke to Adriane.

"It seems he has received a promotion."

"I wonder if it came about following our visit," Adrien added.

In a silent moment, Dieter noticed Hauke rub his leg.

"Are they still sore?"

"Yes, they ache."

"Then wait."

He returned with a large bottle.

"It's a liniment. I found it in a cupboard upstairs when we arrived."

He massaged the boy's calves while Hauke leaned back and smiled, making occasional sounds of happiness.

"Better?" Dieter enquired when he'd finished.

"Oh yes. It's warm. Nice."

"Then I'll repeat the treatment until you're fit enough to do your chores."

"Chores?"

"Yes, this is a farm."

Then, after a brief pause, they laughed.

Slowly as the night wore on their stories intermingled until they looked down the road from their front gate and their story became one.

They all returned to bed to sleep until dawn.

She was at his bedside again. The room was light.

"Hauke, you know when we first met back in Berlin and I mentioned that you needed to bathe?"

Hauke moved up onto one elbow in his bed. He blinked then nodded.

"Well, it's happened again. Come on, the bath is hot and ready."

Casting all protocols aside Adriane did not leave the boy to wash, she knelt over the bath and pushed him down washing every inch of him. She washed his hair twice. Hauke protested a little at first but gave away his pride and infant masculinity for the joy of being treated and cared for by a person who did what they did out of love rather than necessity.

He entered their kitchen wrapped in a towel and was positioned near the stove by Adriane.

"Who is this bright, sparkling child I see before me?" said Dieter, turning his head sideways to look at Hauke's face.

The boy looked back at him and smiled.

"I'm not a child," he muttered.

For a moment Dieter watched him then a look of puzzlement came over his face.

"Hauke, when we first met, I remember you saying that you were twelve years old and would soon be thirteen. How old are you now? When is your birthday?"

Hauke looked down at his fingers, playing them together.

"Oh, yes ..... I lied," he said at last. "I was eleven soon to be twelve.

My birthday is June 16 so this time I will really be thirteen. When is June? It must be soon. Or has it passed."

Dieter looked up. Adriane had a tear in her eye. She had cried a lot in the past twenty-four hours.

Dieter once again lowered his head and turned it to meet the boy's gaze. Then he knelt down and hugged the boy.

"This is remarkable," he said. "Hauke, it is June. Yesterday was the sixteenth."

It took five days to organise. Egon came to inspect the boy returned from the dead. He knew the story. Now he was a witness to the resurrection. He came each day to offer new ideas and more items for the food. Perhaps the loss of his own sons gave him a little impetus to make this one memorable. Hauke seemed to like the old man. They talked incessantly.

Martha would make the cake. She understood the importance of the event. Afterwards, she told them, she would take Adriane to her house and give her some more cooking lessons in her lovely warm, ever active kitchen. She went on a secret trip to a nearby town to seek out fine sugar and chocolate for the icing of her cake.

They invited Egon and Martha, Klaus Muller with his wife Ursula and with their boy Lambert and young Mila.

Also Manfred Schroder with his parents Walter and Ilse. Walter volunteered his wife to supply her famous potato and bacon pies.

Word of the boy from Berlin slipped through the village and spread into the daily gossip.

It was a story with some closure even if it involved three people who had lost everything and everybody.

Interest grew.

Parties and celebration were something that people had put aside, as if such a thing would be considered poor form in these hard times. Also, there was a certain degree of shame. The people of Germany were divided by a line of reasoning which for the faithful saw their loss as a crooked, cruel turn of fate whereas the realists accepted their crime and wished to present a level of contrition to the occupying forces. This situation was different. There was a story of redemption attached. The gathering was on the edge of the town on a farm. Who would notice?

"I think I had a birthday party when I was very young," Hauke mentioned looking about brightly. "This will be the first one I will remember."

Chapter 19

'Celebration'

This day had a sparkle to it. As if polished and especially lustrous.
It was to be a lunchtime gathering. The attendees were asked just to bring some food or drink if they could spare something. By 11am the Kingeles and the Schroders were already placing bowls and platters on the tables in the barn.

Adriane and Dieter gave Hauke a handsome large hardbound book full of blank lined pages plus an ornate fountain pen. Adriane found both items at the post office. The lady in the post office fondly remembered Hauke and explained how she worried about him after he left on the day he had asked about his 'friends'. It seemed Hauke's quest was now well known.
She was so pleased to hear of his good fortune that Adriane invited her and her husband to the party. In return, Lena

Koch gave Adriane a good discount on her purchase.
"I've had those items for some time," she confessed. "I'm
glad the lad will get some use out of them. He can write
down all his adventures. I call them adventures. Trials may
have been the appropriate word."

After Adriane mentioned she had invited the people from
the post office, Dieter confessed that he had invited the man
from the shop where he bought nails, screws and items for
farm repairs.
"Their names are Markus and Antje Keller. They have a
daughter called Gerde. She's seven. Their son is six. His
name is Dolph. Markus is ex Wehrmacht. He was the one
who gave Hauke our address. We owe them that much."
Adriane looked at her husband.
"Well, men are gossips too, it would seem. I'm sure they'll
be very nice. It's good that we are meeting people and good
for Hauke. I hope we have enough food to keep everybody
happy."
Then she added.
"Hans Koch said he will bring beer. Perhaps he has some
bottles."

When presented with his birthday gift Hauke had quietly run
his fingers over the fat book with over one hundred rules
pages on heavy cream paper and seemed genuinely pleased.
He took his new fountain pen and at the top of the first page
he wrote 'Hauke', then he hesitated.
Dieter picked up on the moment. An ideal chance.
"You can write 'Kluge' if you like however, please know that it
is my wish and Adriane's wish that you will soon be our son.

You will have a family once more. We will complete whatever paperwork is needed to make the whole process official. If you agree then your last name will be Falke. Does that idea appeal to you?"

Hauke looked at Dieter then Adriane. His eyes were lost in troubles. He looked away.
"In some time soon ..... I'm not good with these things."
He pointed to Adriane's distended abdomen.
"You will be having a baby. It will be your very own child. I am an outcast. Will I still be welcome? I want to be sure."
Dieter looked at his wife. He was amazed that the boy could have any doubts regarding their love for him. Still, he felt he understood. A twelve-year-old is still a child. In a normal life, reassurance and certainty and belonging are all part of day to day existence. Hauke had all these normalities ripped away from him. Nothing in his world was certain. Nothing could be trusted completely. He resisted the urge to hold Hauke.
Instead, he took his face in his hands.
"Listen to me. Your life has been very hard. Sad and cruel. Leaving you in Berlin will haunt me all my days. It was your will and your fortitude that has brought us together once more. Our love for you is unconditional. Perhaps you don't understand how much. When the baby is born it will be your little sister or brother. If other children follow they too will be part of our family. You are part of us, part of our story. You are as much a part as if you were born right here. Nobody will ever let you down again."
Dieter let go of Hauke's face. He looked into the boy's eyes. Adriane with one hand over her mouth simply reached out

and touched Hauke's arm.

He sat for some seconds as if absorbing Dieter's fine words. He closed his eyes and bowed his head slightly then he took up his pen and in his new book wrote a second word, 'Falke'.

It was Adriane's intention to explain to Hauke that a note-book she had been carrying for him had provided the key evidence to the Americans that opened the way to the farm and their happiness. In the end, she left the tale for another day. Adoption, after all, was enough for the boy to absorb for the moment.

Outside, people were gathering. They gave a little cheer when Hauke ventured into the yard.
"Who are the two men drinking beer?" Dieter asked as he approached the barn.
"I don't know them," Adriane replied.
As if on queue Walter Schroder stepped up and gave a smile that hinted of great satisfaction.
"Such a lovely day. I hope you do not mind. I needed help so I brought along Boden and Gerrit. I've recently employed them to help with my piggery. It seems Germany wants pork so I'm expanding. They are ex regular soldiers with nowhere to go."
Dieter held out his hands.
"Of course that is fine. They are welcome. Why did you need help here today?"
"Ahhh," said Walter. "With my pig of course. People must eat."
The man guided Dieter and Adriane to the barn. At one side,

near the door a quite sizeable pig was glistening in golden perfection on a spit. The two men where taking turns in the basting and turning.

"Good God." Adriane was tugging Dieter's sleeve.

"Look at this place."

The barn was filled with food. Hans Koch had supplied beer as promised but not a few bottles, instead, a half-barrel with a tap. The Muller's contribution was baskets of apples and other fruit, apple pies, strudel plus carefully labelled vats of cider. One said, 'Alkohol' the other said, 'Für die Kinder. Kein Alkohol'.

"There are other people I don't know," Adriane whispered. Dieter laughed.

"Well, it appears, food is the price of entry. That's the town baker and there are several baskets of bread. Nobody will starve or go thirsty. What can we do? Let's enjoy the occasion and see where it goes."

The party lasted throughout the afternoon and into the evening. Indeed many unknown people appeared. They all brought offerings. Some generous, others what they could spare. The atmosphere was cheerful. A reason to grasp life again and perhaps with less shame, find a little happiness in company and hospitality.

Dieter noticed as he moved about that there was virtually no mention of the catastrophic war they had just endured. Whether it was collective guilt or a wish to move on, to walk away from the recent past, he was not sure. The crowd appeared to be at ease but there was no spontaneous laughter or exuberant behaviour. It was as if they were cautious in case their gathering was inappropriate.

Hauke was brought forward at one stage and made to cut his cake and taste it and give his approval. Which he did amongst much laughter. The crowd sang songs to him while men shook his hand and women gave him hugs. He looked a little overwhelmed as the well-meaning guests surrounded the boy with a story.
Dieter stepped forward and gently extricated him from the throng to steer him away round the side of the house and out of sight. He found Mila and the Schroder's teenage boy Manfred and asked them to keep him company, adding the Muller's little six-year-old lad, Lambert, as they walked.
Half an hour later when he checked they were sitting in a tight little group chatting happily and eating a small picnic they had gathered for themselves. They had been joined by the Keller's children. Dieter watched them secretly for some minutes, enjoying the scene of some happy, innocent children, little aware of history.
If the world ever forgives us he thought, Germany may have a future.

In the darkness. at the end of the proceedings, the town baker offered those few that were still about, transport back to town in his van. With final handshakes and waves, they departed and only the farm's immediate neighbours were left. The men and women stood about contemplating all that had taken place.
"What a day," said Egon, hands on his hips. "I did not expect this to happen. It seems people needed an excuse to gather and risk a little enjoyment. Hauke was the key."

Dieter looked at his friends, his eyebrows raised.

"There's still food in the barn. We must share it out. Incidentally, where are the children?"

Walter chuckled.

"I went looking for Manfred. He's asleep on your floor. Hauke is asleep next to him. Mila and Lambert are asleep on the lounge. I suspect they all tried the beer or the 'cider for adults'. Possibly both."

"It is perhaps the nicest part of the day," said Ilse Schroder. When the others looked puzzled, she added, "That the children, despite their age variance, all appear to like each other's company. I would like to think they will all travel to school each day together."

Only Egon and Martha Kingele remained silent. With their two sons lost in the war, there was little of the conversation that brought them comfort. Klaus quietly patted Egon's shoulder.

It was agreed that the barn doors be shut and they would meet again in the morning to clear things away. Boden and Gerrit had left earlier. They would return to assist in moving the pig spit back to the Schroder's farm.

The children were woken and walked in a fog of sleep out the door into the night. Hauke stumbled to his bed and immediately fell asleep once more.

"That is the sleep of a drunkard," Dieter said to Adriane. "We'll have to watch that boy. He may develop a liking for such liquids."

As he left the room Dieter noticed a box near Hauke's bed. "What's that?" he whispered."

Once more in their parlour, Adriane answered.

"It was from Lena Koch. They're books. She apologised for not bringing food. I reminded her that her husband supplied all that beer. Apparently, he is close friends with the owner of the rathskeller. She bought a gift for Hauke instead. The books are quite wonderful. Shakespeare, Fontane, Wolfe, Kafka … "

"That's some heavy reading for a thirteen-year-old."

"She admitted that. She said that any boy who could do what Hauke had done must be resourceful and intelligent. She hopes he will appreciate them someday. She said that she had bought them all for her children but that was not to be. It was quite sad really."

Dieter hugged his wife.

"I hope she is right. It would be good if our eldest child is well-read and scholarly."

He then held his wife out from him to look at her face.

"I heard that the Koch's only returned to their Post Office last year. They were missing for quite some time during the war. I didn't enquire as to why. People are touchy about the past."

Chapter 20

'The Truck'

As agreed, the neighbours all returned in the morning.
Supplies of leftover bread, cheese, sausage and pastries were
divided up and placed in boxes or sacks.
The beer and alcoholic cider had all been drained so they
sat for a while and sipped the last of the kinder cider so that
Klaus could take away his containers.
Egon suggested that he would need his truck to return the
beer barrel to the rathskeller. He would also take some food
to Hans and Lena Koch at their post office.
"Because you do not have a truck," he added with an odd
look on his face.
Dieter was about to enquire about such a look when Hauke
wandered out of the house rubbing his face and looking
about with half-closed eyes.
"I think our son has discovered the bad side of adult drinks,"
Adriane observed. "He may leave them alone for some years

now."

The boy wandered across to the adults sitting just inside the barn doors. He seated himself next to Adriane and gave a quiet sigh, his head in his hands.

"Good morning, Hauke," said Walter. "I trust you slept well, after your party."

Hauke made a soft non-committal sound, not even raising his head.

Adriane nudged him.

"Go to the kitchen. Make coffee with milk and have warm bread. You'll feel better."

Hauke stood, his head to one side. He made another noise and walked slowly back to the house.

Ursula Muller watched him depart.

"All our children are in the same state. I scolded Mila for letting Lambert drink beer. She said he enjoyed it so much she couldn't stop him. He's still asleep."

Dieter looked round at his friends. He had a request.

"You may have heard me speak of Hauke as our son. It seems an obvious next step. We wish to make it official. Does anybody know how and where an adoption process begins?"

Nobody knew but the general opinion was that with the recent terrible events, there would be many, many needs for adoption and the relocation of children. The process would be either painfully slow and endless or for expediency perhaps simpler and quite fast.

The Willingen council and committee it was decided, was too involved in local civil matters such as rebuilding and restoring basic services. Paperwork was not their strong-point.

Finally, the group suggested that the answer may lie
with Lena and Hans Koch at the Post Office. They were
long-standing local residents and handled a great deal of
official forms and correspondence.
Adriane was pleased with at least some idea of where the
answer may lie. She would call into the post office the first
chance she had.
In the silence that followed the decision, Martha Kingele
lowered her head and said, "It was a terrible thing. What
happened to them. Unforgivable. How they survived I do not
know. They have my utmost respect."

There it was again. A reference to those people from the post
office. A 'terrible thing'? What could that mean?"
Dieter prepared himself to ask the question when Boden and
Gerrit walked in to help with the pig spit. The moment was
lost.

The two men loaded the spit onto the Schroder's wagon and
then with the two farmhands sitting with their legs over the
back tray and the family in the front they moved off.
Klaus and Ursula Muller boarded their truck with the cider
casks and fruit baskets in the back and also headed out the
gate.
Dieter and Egon watched them go.
"Those two farmhands are not very talkative," Dieter observed.
"Ah, they're just quiet fellows. I've seen them chatting and
laughing together. They seem to enjoy each others company.
Perhaps they spent time together in the war."
"They don't talk about it," said Dieter. "I tried to ask about

their background. They were rather non-committal. Then I
must consider that I have no family left, neither does my wife
or my new son. War-time experiences can be painful.”

“My point has been made,” said Egon.
He lifted his hand to his eyes to view the departing vehicle.
“Nice truck. They are very lucky to have a truck to sit on.
Not everybody has a truck.”
The little man continued to stare at the truck in the distance.
In the silence, Dieter had to ask.
“Egon, you’re a fine friend and a wonderful neighbour but I
have noticed of late you continue to make pointed remarks
about trucks and more to the point, my lack of such a piece
of equipment. Can I ask, to what end?”
For some moments Egon stood his ground then as if over-
come, he turned and burst out laughing.
“I kept thinking. Is Dieter missing my remarks? Is he too
polite to ask?”
He put his hand on Dieter’s arm.
“I have a story which will please you. If it is true. Listen. My
eldest son had a very close friend. We knew him well. They
grew up together. They went to war together. My son’s friend
survived. He is employed locally. He is now, under the guidance of the Americans, in charge in this area for one thing.
He handles the disposal of war equipment. He was a prisoner
for a short time until they were all released to return home.
They kept some POWs and gave them a kind of job. He is
even paid. I met him in the town last week. We reminisced.
He is not the wonderful cheerful chap who drank and chased
girls with my son. But he is trying to start his life over. Then
he said the most amazing thing. Can you guess? Can you

guess?"

"Something to do with trucks."

"Yes, yes," said Egon, waving arms in front of him.

"He said, almost casually, do you need a motorbike or a truck, Egon? I have quite a number. They're for sale or at my discretion, I can give them to local communities. Staff cars are scrutinised, as are weapons, practically forbidden but not trucks and motorbikes."

Egon paused, to take a breath, then continued his story.

"We are to visit the compound in two days time. He will arrange for some of the best vehicles to be available for us to view. For the sake of his paperwork, we are from a farming cooperative. So you are my assistant. If there are enough vehicles then I will mention this to Herr Muller and Herr Schroder but first I wish to have a nice new vehicle for myself plus a very useful addition to my good friend Dieter's farm."

Egon was ebullient.

"What do you say?"

"I say, wonderful," said Dieter.

Chapter 21

'Vehicles'

The yard was large. Thirty kilometres from Willingen.
It covered several fields next to a small American infantry
unit. They had tents and buildings on the edges. The area
was surrounded by a high wire fence. At the gate, Egon mentioned his contact's name and was ushered through without
much interest.
He parked near what looked like an administration hut.
There were rows of trucks, half-tracks, cars and the paraphernalia of war. In the distance, men could be seen disman-
tling large guns. There were many piles of steel and smaller
piles of brass and copper waiting for a return to use in some
other form.
Egon sat and stared.
"A lot of vehicles. But they all look as if they were in a battle
.... and lost."
He shrugged his shoulders.

"Oh well, I'll see if I can find our man. Lot of Americans about. I hope they don't interfere."

As Egon walked away, Dieter alighted from their truck. Egon had splashed mud all over it and done his best to make the machine look old and battered and thus in need of replacement.

Hauke had asked to come along for the ride and now Dieter called him down from the cab. He planned a visit to the Post Office on the way back so having the boy with him may help.

Two Americans walked past. They said 'Hi' in a casual but not necessarily friendly manner. No interest was shown. The trucks really did look in bad shape. Some even had bullet and shrapnel holes in the doors and bonnets. Windows were shattered and some had scorch marks from fire. Egon appeared from the building he had entered. With him was a young man carrying a clipboard. After introductions, he pointed at the nearby trucks.

"In case you're concerned, these vehicles here are too badly damaged. They are all to be scrapped. Come with me."

The group walked down rows of trucks and cars. As they progressed the condition of the items on display improved. While well-worn the trucks looked usable. The man stopped.

"These are quite big beasts. They've seen a lot of work but if you want a really big machine then they are available. Be warned they use a lot of fuel. I'm thinking what I have to show you next may be what you'll like."

They walked on and then cut through between some of the trucks into a slightly open area. In it there were about ten trucks and a row of motorbikes. Egon's eyes lit up. The young man smiled.

"I thought this might be more to your liking Egon, you father of my best friend. These are Mercedes L3000. They're 3-tonne. You can have tray-side or full covered back. They were new near the end of the war. Hardly any use. They are army trucks. The reason they are dark blue or dark brown is because the Americans insist we paint them before they can be released. So as not to cause any alarm if they're seen driving about."

Egon walked over and touched the nearest truck smiling broadly.

"Any of these?"

"Yes. I decided to be honest with the Americans. I explained my relationship with you and how I would like to help you. For a moment I thought I had made a mistake then the American said that his 'Daddy' was a farmer and as long as I made the paperwork all look right he didn't want to know. My suggestion is that you and Dieter choose a truck each then we'll hide a motorbike on the back for each of you."

They looked the trucks over. Dieter chose a blue tray-side and after much walking to and fro Egon decided on a brown truck with a full with a complete rear cab.

"I'm thinking of you," he said to Dieter. "If you need to keep items from the weather then you can borrow my truck."

With the motorbikes, Dieter chose a shiny BMW R71 while Egon picked a BMW R75 with a sidecar. The trucks were topped up with diesel from drums rolled over by other German workers.

The motorbikes were fuelled up and loaded into the covered truck for less scrutiny.

It was decided that Egon's old truck would be delivered back to his farm by one of the staff following along.

"Now," said their benefactor, "what shall we put on the sale document."

Back at the office, it was decided that they would be called the 'Hugel Bauernhof Gruppe'.

"That sounds cooperative," opined Egon, "and there is a hill near us."

As they left to collect their vehicles, the two Americans who had walked past earlier stopped in front of them.

"Hold on a minute," he said. His German was understandable.

"I thought it was you, now I'm sure."

He stood with his hands on his hips.

Egon and Dieter exchanged nervous glances.

"What is the problem?" asked Egon.

The large American looked at him as if puzzled.

"Oh, no problem." He advanced on Hauke. He squinted.

"This little fella. We met him a while back, trudging into town. He looked beat. We took his case and coat for him. Hey, looks like you found them people you was lookin' for."

Hauke's eyes were wide.

"Yes, I did. Thank you for your help. I .. I made it."

"Well that's great," said the American. "You had us a little worried. Good to hear."

They left, after giving Hauke a handshake and another bar of chocolate.

"Chocolate and trucks," said Egon. "It is indeed a fine day."

He tasted a piece of Hauke's chocolate.

"Though we Germans, I feel, used to make better chocolate.

Perhaps we will again."

Shortly after their departure the large American Sergeant
who had spoken to Hauke placed a call to one of the Army
Intelligence Units. When the operator answered he said,
"Yeah Hi, this is Sergeant Hurley from the 14th transport
detail near Willingen. Can you give a message to Colonel
Yates. Can you tell that further to his inquiry. Tell him, the
kid made it. He'll know what that means."

At the outskirts of Willingen Egon turned off toward their
farms while Dieter changed gears with a little difficulty and
drove into the town.
"I haven't driven many trucks," he said, in reply to Hauke's
quizzical look.
They stopped near the Post Office and entered. A woman
was sending a letter.
'Danke, Frau Koch."
She smiled and nodded as she left.
Lena Koch called out to the back of the shop.
"Hans. It's Dieter and little Hauke. Come and say hullo."
When the two people behind the counter were about to ask
what they could do for their customers Dieter said his piece.
"I'd like to thank you for your generosity in attending the
birthday gathering. It was most appreciated. I hope you en-
joyed the day."
On cue, Hauke added.
"And I thank you very much for the books. I've never had
many books of my own."
Hans Koch nodded at the boy.
"I know they do not appear too exciting to you at the mo-

ment but in time, as your learning progresses you will hopefully appreciate what you find in them."

A momentary silence ensued.

"It was kind of you to call in with your thanks. We appreciate your effort. Was there something else?" asked Lena.

"Yes, yes there is." Dieter put his arm on his boy's shoulder.

"Do you have the papers required for an adoption."

"Oh of course. Yes, we do. I'd imagine they are still valid. I doubt a war changes such things. Except perhaps the need for more forms."

The woman hesitated.

"We looked into the procedure once ourselves. But at that time there were no orphans available."

The papers were found. They were complex. They involved references, photos, interviews, health checks, proof of abode and income, racial background.

In the end, Lena Koch snatched them up.

"This will not do. It has all come back to me. Such a procedure could not possibly still be in operation. The country needs expediency, not obstacles. War is a friend to no one. Please, Dieter, leave this matter with me. I will make enquiries. I will make it work for you."

Dieter thanked the two people, then as he was about to leave he added a line which he thought might be suitable.

"The war was terrible for us all. I believe you both suffered in some way because of it."

It was as if he had cursed the devil. A darkness descended on the room. Not in a physical sense but in the atmosphere surrounding the occupants.

Lena and Hans Koch stood still. Frozen by the words.

Hauke had not moved, sensing something was not right.

Dieter looked about then tried to speak.

"I .... I'm sorry ..... I hope I have not caused offence ... "

Hans Koch shook his head.

"It's okay Dieter. I assume you do not know. You're not from here."

He paused, as if deciding whether he should proceed.

"So, let me ask you something. Since you have mentioned this subject we would like to know a little ourselves. This town is not perhaps the pleasant place you see. I mean as an outsider, newly arrived in our midst. You deserve to know. However, there are still a lot of people about with a past that they may wish to keep in the past. You seem a very nice fellow. Would you mind terribly if we confirm that?"

He stopped momentarily, then added.

"If we ascertain that you are the sort of person we think you are then we would like to unburden ourselves to you. It will all be in the strictest of confidences. Do you agree to this?"

Chapter 22

'The Past'

They gave Hauke some cake and coffee and asked him to
stay at the counter and call if a customer entered.

In the back of the shop in their parlour Lena then Hans
began to ask Dieter Falke about his life. They seemed quite
intent. Once started the questions were endless. They wanted to hear of his upbringing, his parents, his brother, his
schooling, his affiliations. It soon became apparent that all
the time the questions were moving closer to his opinions
of his country, the Government, the Nazi Party, the Schutzstaffel, the Fuhrer and finally the destruction of human life
by means of the death camps. Was he in favour of wiping out
races of people such as gypsies and Jews?
Early in the discussions as he was peppered with questions
Dieter decided that whatever these Koch people wanted to
know he would tell the truth. He was increasingly concerned

that he was dealing with some hidden remnants of Nazi
fanaticism and that his answers would forever condemn any
association he had with these people.

Still, he went ahead. Once started he found that he could
not stop. Like a man condemning himself with his words the
story just unfolded.

He told them that he abhorred the monstrous crimes carried out by his fellow Germans in their quest to exterminate
millions of humans and that the stain of these acts would
forever blight his country. As an honourable German he had
joined the army. In the early days of the Fuhrer he was impressed by how the country was energised and appeared to
prosper. However, as his fighting unit was plunged into more
and more insane, reckless adventures which had no strategic
or military purpose it became apparent that the Fuhrer and
his cohorts had lost all ability for rational thought. He and
his fellow soldiers realised that they were no longer fighting
for a strong Germany and a better world, they were fighting
for simple survival at the whim of a desperate man.
Unfortunately, many decent Wehrmacht soldiers died during
this time. Even when their situation was hopeless. When
Germany was lost and there was no point to any of it, the
crazed fanatics of the Waffen SS urged them on with curses
and threats.

He ended the war with nearly all his friends and comrades
and all his family dead about him and a deep distrust of all
people.

"I am no longer proud to be German but I cannot change who
I am so I accept that life goes on. My only saviour is that I
am blessed with the company of Adriane and Hauke. If I have

offended you and your beliefs then that must be the way it is. Should you wish me to leave now I will go.”

It was Lena Koch who spoke first.
“No, please do not leave.”
Just then Hauke called that there was a customer in the shop.
As Lena went to attend to the post office Hans said, “I’d rather wait till Lena returns, so that we can speak together.”

Seated once more Lena moved forward in her chair.
“Dieter, what you saw at your gathering two days ago was just one side of this place. This town is not all the pleasant community you may, as a newcomer, envisage. There are a number of sympathisers still amongst us.”
Hans Koch joined in.
“Yes, Dieter, to clarify our position. We were missing for some time during the war. We were sent away to a prison camp. Those who knew us as friends did not expect to ever see us again.
We were betrayed and condemned by some of our fellow citizens. The main perpetrators of our downfall were the previous owners of the farm where you now live. They were the head of the local party branch. They saw it as their absolute duty to find anybody who gave even a hint of disloyalty to Nazism and have them removed. Others went missing. Unlike us, they did not return. By a series of fateful moves that may have been paperwork or intentional we eventually were sent all the way to Poland, to Auschwitz.
We were separated and just waited to die. Many times we managed not to be chosen.

In a place so horrible that perhaps those who died there were the lucky ones."

"The Russians saved us," added Lena.

"We were marched out, to move us to Germany. The Russian army was coming. They walked us through the snow. I think the idea was that we would mostly die. The SS took great delight in killing the Jews. Those that stopped through weakness or lack of will received a bullet in the back of the head. Often they would push them over in the snow and then say, 'You are too weak' and shoot them. We were German and yet we were going to suffer the same fate. There was no pity. Until we started marching I did not know that Hans was still alive. He saw me and caught up. Hans said we would surely die if we didn't get away from the march.

As we walked round a bend where the snow was banked deep on the steep lower side of the road Hans threw a rock at a drift above us. Miraculously his idea worked. The snow dropped with a thump. Everybody looked. He pushed me off the road down into some deep snow then jumped after me. It buried us. It hid us. A Jew walking behind looked straight into my eyes and mouthed the words 'Viel Glück.'

I will not trouble you with how we came to be back in Willingen except to say that a Polish farmer with so many reasons for hate, fed us and resurrected us out of pure kindness. His family gave us clothes and a chance to make our way back into Germany and by various means, we travelled all the way to our home.

It was our intention to seek revenge on the people who had done these things to us but American bombers saved us the trouble. A direct hit on the party meeting in the town wiped them out. Is that not divine providence?"

The story had stopped. All three people in the room sat gathering their thoughts.

"So you simply voiced opinions against the National Socialists?" asked Dieter.

"For a while, it was tolerated."

Hans shook his head as if denying his actions.

"We were too naive. Those people from your farm. I will not speak their name. They called in the Geheime Staatspolizei. Gave them a list. It happened in the night. Homes were raided and in the morning many were gone. The war was starting to go badly in places.. Those Gestapo thugs were edgy and desperate. They wanted to blame anybody. Some I believe were shot. Others like us were simply thrown into the camp transports."

Dieter lifted his hand to his forehead.

"In Berlin, they were hanging any who they doubted the cause, even children. We were and probably still are, a country divided."

He looked at Lena and Hans. They seemed to be glancing at each other as if in an odd silent discussion.

Dieter asked.

"Is there something more you wish me to know or something you would rather I did not know. I feel you've told me your story for a reason."

"Forgive us," said Hans. "It takes a long time to begin trusting again. In this case, it is a question of ethics. You are well-liked Dieter but you are new to this town. Should we involve you in an activity that is not of your concern? It has been discussed and we are still not clear. Perhaps we should not

have told you our story but we were intrigued to know your
loyalties. Now we can report back."
Dieter was curious.
"Report back to whom?"
"To your neighbours. The Kingeles, the Mullers and most
importantly to the Schroders."
"So they were all against the National Socialists?"
"Yes, but more discreet than us. Egon had the hardest job,
living next door to the local party chief. When Egon's two
sons were killed in the endless war he became quite bitter."
Dieter decided to be more direct.
"Your story is compelling. In turn, someday I will fill in the
missing details of how and why Adriane and I arrived here.
That aside, I repeat, I have the feeling that this discussion
is all for a reason. What is it you're not telling me. What is it
you want to know."
Lena lowered her voice.
"We are seeking help, Dieter. There is something that needs
to be done. We are not sure what action to take. First, it must
involve seeking information."
The post office lady lowered her voice.
"Those two men, the ones working at the Schroder's piggery.
They are not former Wehrmacht soldiers. When I saw them
at your farm I remembered them. They are SS Einsatzgruppen. They worked at Auschwitz."

Chapter 23

'Decisions and Deception'

"You were listening weren't you?"

Dieter looked at the silent boy sitting beside him as they drove to the farm. His head was down in thought.

"Yes," he said, after some hesitation. Then he asked, "Will you do it?"

"I have to consider our future Hauke. Should I risk it or just let the past stay in the past. There are options to consider."

"How bad were these 'camps'? Did they actually kill lots of people there?"

Dieter glanced at Hauke. The boy was serious.

"We Germans murdered hundreds of thousands. Possibly a lot more, I'm still not sure of the numbers. As the truth slowly comes out and the perpetrators are punished we will know all the story. It's okay that you didn't know. How could you?"

"If these men are just two more of the camp workers why are

they special?"

"Frau Koch thinks they were more than that. She thinks they were heavily involved in the killing and she heard stories of terrible crimes they committed. She's right, of course.
We need to know or it will be a sore that will not heal."

Lena and Hans Koch had revealed that how days before Hauke's birthday gathering Walter Schroder called to see them. He was concerned about the two men he had employed to help on his farm. He hoped he was wrong.
His son Manfred was working with the men feeding the pigs. One had laughed at one of the pigs and said that it looked like a 'Juden'.
"What method should we use," they joked. Then they looked at him and fell silent.
Another day when they were eating lunch he brought them some water in a jug. Unaware of his approach he heard them comparing the 'gas' or the 'spritze'. They ceased talking when they saw him.
Walter suspected these men may have lied to him about their part in the war and what they did may have been much more sinister.
As an anti-fascist, it troubled him that he could be harbouring men who might be criminals even by the standards of war but he wanted to be sure. For the time being, he would hold his opinion.
He would bring them to Hauke's celebration and pretend that all was well.

Now they were more concerned. After Lena recognised these men as having worked at Auschwitz, the old group wanted to know details of their participation in that place. Certainly, they were not Wehrmacht. They must be SS and nobody who worked at such a place could claim to be of good character. Lena Koch was certain they were two who were rumoured to have carried out some of the most vile crimes in the camp. But she was not sure. Camp rumours could be wrong. Many were untrue. If they were wrong then it could be forgotten. What would they do if true?

How could they extract information?

It was here that they asked Dieter if he would be willing to try a ruse whereby he befriended the two men and quietly advised them that he was really SS and worked on the transports. In other words, he sent the victims to their extermination camp. They felt that such a kinship may motivate them to talk about what their role was at the other end of the train line.

It seemed a workable plan.

Obviously, it meant a lot to his neighbours and the two people at the post office. Perhaps capturing two mass murderers would give them all some satisfaction and closure. They could move on.

The Americans had made announcements to the effect that they were seeking death camp operatives and harbouring such people would be unwise. Do they tell the Americans? Would this cause unease in the town, if they betrayed some fellow Germans? What else could they do? Just drive these men away?

At night, with their boy asleep, Dieter talked at length to his wife. Nothing could excuse the systematic murder of so many people. She agreed. He explained in detail, the story of

the neighbours and their anti-fascist sentiments. The intern-
ment of many from the town. Hatred, lies, deceit, betrayal.
It would be the right thing to do. He took the hand of his wife
as they sat on the lounge with its rose-coloured tapestry
covering.

"I feel I owe our friends this help. We have a new life here.
There are so many good people. How could we harbour
murderers? I doubt there any Jewish people about. The local
fanatics would have hunted them down and shipped them
away."

Dieter paused as if he had spoken out of turn. Adriane's face
was lost in some far off place. She looked scared.

He reached out and touched her belly.

"It needs to be a good place for our new child. But I will not
go ahead unless you agree. Please, do you have any doubts?"

The young woman looked across the room to the walls, the
floor, the building that they now owned. Since their arrival,they had made an effort to hide signs of the previous occupants. Partly to make the place their own but also to remove
reminders of what these people stood for in their blind Nazi
beliefs.

None of the paraphernalia of the Fuhrer's Germany could be
found in the house when they took up occupancy. She suspected Egon, kind, decent Egon.

Practical useful things remained but nothing that would
cause offence. Egon did mention that the Americans had
accompanied him on an inspection when they gave him the
key, as part of their sweep of the areas for assets to be used
by them. They confiscated some jewellery and valuables as
war reparations but left everything else untouched.

She considered the fortunes that brought them all together.

The tragedy for each of them, the loss of everything and everybody they each had. Somehow three people abandoned by the world and its events, found one another and now by some odd fortune were on the brink of a fair future.

Dieter sat waiting beside his wife. He did not interrupt her reverie.

She turned to him.

"All the decisions we've made so far have seen us through. Do your best my husband."

Chapter 24

'Revelations'

"Guten Tag meine Freunde."

"Guten Tag, Dieter."

Boden and Gerrit both looked up and waved. They were taking their time clearing some land for a new storage building at the corner of Schroder's piggery.

In his increasing visits to the farm, Dieter learnt that the two men were affable, conceited, of only fair intelligence and vague about their past. Dropping odd pieces of commentary into their conversation concerning days past and life in the battlefield brought forth a great deal of flustering and changes of subject. There was a wall between them.

Eventually, in turn, he left small hints that perhaps his past as a Wehrmacht soldier may not be entirely factual.

Though as yet they had not picked up on any of this pretext. It was their gregarious attitude that he would exploit.

He suspected that once he broke through their guard and

established some common background they would not be able to stop from boasting about their exploits. Today was to be the day that he would announce his false SS credentials. First he would unleash, accidentally, a series of remarks concerning his hatred of the Jews. With his knowledge of Adriane and his feelings of humanity, it would go against his core being but he reconciled the greater good of his actions with the possible results.

His rank would be reasonably high. It would allay doubts as to his loyalty and purpose while instilling a certain respect. Hopefully, they would answer questions because of a previous inbuilt necessity to obey a senior official.

He thought for some time about what level of command he should be in order to be a safely higher rank while not being so grand so as to make his story suspicious.

He finally settled on being a Hauptsturmführer. A middle command with some authority but still close enough to the day to day workings to be interested in whatever his targets may wish to divulge.

His visits to see Walter and Ilse Schroder involved his supposed skills as an architectural draftsman. He would be advising on the new buildings. This meant he spent time walking about, making notes, taking measurements and thus engaging with the two workers.

In turn, the son Manfred was to stay inside to attend to his studies leaving Dieter to participate in long conversations in a safe environment without fear of being overheard or interrupted.

From the Schroder's kitchen, Dieter and Walter looked through the lace curtains at the two men very slowly levelling the soil near the rear fence.

"There is no urgency in their work," commented Walter.

"They seem to do just enough to appear active."

Dieter placed a large roll of sheets of paper on the table.

"My plans for you to check."

"Blank as usual."

"Yes, but they saw me carrying them in. Now I shall take a large tape measure and three cups of coffee down to the worksite. There's a cool breeze blowing. I'll suggest they take a break and we shelter in the entrance to the nearest shed."

Walter went to their stove to retrieve a large kettle.

"I'll prepare the coffee. The rest is up to you."

As Dieter sat with Boden and Gerrit he decided that he must start and control the conversation. As an Oberleutnant in his Wehrmacht regiment, he knew how to talk to men.

"This is better," he'd said as they arrived. "No point having a warm drink in cold weather. Somewhere to shelter. To take stock. Did you find that in your days in the field?"

The response was muttered.

He let a silence fall over the group as they sat and sipped the coffee. Time to take charge.

He looked both men up and down making it quite obvious he was taking stock of what he saw. He stared.

Enough to elicit a response even if only subliminally.

He hoped his manner was that of somebody in charge. They glanced at him. Were they nervous?

"You know .... he said, at last, leaving a suitable pause.

"You do not strike me as men who have seen combat. Battle leaves its marks. Soldiers who have been there. They have the signs. A weariness, a measure of the dread and the fear.

You have none. It is not so.”

He waited. Let the words hang in the air. Then, after a practised amount of time, he continued.

“Perhaps I’m just better at hiding the facts than you two chaps. It is a talent I have. A talent I think you lack.”

“What do you mean?” asked Boden almost reluctantly.

At last. They had made a move. Time to plunge in.

“Oh come now,” said Dieter. “I can spot the language of the body, the way you carry yourselves, your demeanour.

You have class. Elegance. Don’t be reticent. We’re friends here. Keeping quiet, I understand. You’re one of us aren’t you?”

This was the moment. Dieter waited.

Finally, Boden spoke. His voice was low.

“Are you saying you’re .... “

Plunge in.

“Schutzstaffel. Yes. Of course I am. My instincts are right surely. I’m never wrong. It was an aspect of my command. He’s right of course they would say. You also are SS.”

Now he had made his move Dieter drove home his advantage.

“Don’t be concerned. What is your story? Me, I was in transport. As a Hauptsturmführer in charge of a unit, we moved about sorting and arranging the Jew shipments. Mostly in Poland. Though many came from Germany as well.”

Dieter decided to leave room for a response. Would they still be wary? His two companions both had their cups paused near their mouths. It was almost comical. This time Gerrit spoke.

“Mein Gott, Sir. We did not know.”

He looked happy, relieved. As if a barrier about his person

had suddenly dropped and he was free.

Dieter was shocked. Could it be this easy?

"Did you ship to Auschwitz and Birkenau? asked Gerrit"

Dieter knew he must press on while he had momentum.

"Of course, that was our main task. We could not move the accursed Jews out there fast enough. Why do you ask? Were you in the area?"

Gerrit was almost standing. He leaned forward excitedly. His reaction childish.

"We were there, Sir. What you shipped in we destroyed. You were very good. We were working to capacity. This is incredible. We are both from Auschwitz. We did the final work. What an honour it is to meet a fellow officer, Sir. Indeed an honour."

Dieter now hesitated. He had expected a more drawn out session or series of sessions to extract the truth. The Americans, the British, the French, the Russians were all hunting down these very people. Momentarily he suspected that he was being trapped. Could these men be so stupid? But they continued to talk, to almost babble.

"I am Scharführer Gerrit Klein. This is Scharführer Boden Meler. We used other names with Herr Schroder. Sir, with your commitment to the Jewish solution you will be delighted to hear of some of our methods. If you have the time. The volumes we achieved were remarkable. All with the minimum of fuss. None of them knew that they were being processed. They were like sheep under our control. We are quite proud of the work we carried out. Our methods were, if I might say with modesty, quite groundbreaking and most rewarding."

Both men stood in unison and snapped their heals together.

Before they could raise their arms in salute Dieter ordered them to be seated.

"It is best you do not do that," he suggested. "These are troubled times. Caution is everything. Perhaps return to your work now. At your lunch break, I will join you again. I am most anxious to hear of your work."

He stood in his best stiffened officer pose, nodded briefly and departed.

He kept his head high as he walked away, wondering what gut-wrenching revelations awaited him at their next meeting.

Chapter 25

'Knowing'

Adriane and Dieter Falke decided to walk to the Muller farm. The distance was not great and they needed time to come to terms with what they were about to reveal to their neighbours.
The time was past 10pm and the children were asleep. Adriane assured her husband that walking would not affect her advanced pregnancy. It would be good for them to breath some clean night air.
They were to report to an assembly of local people, their neighbours and others on what information Dieter had obtained over the past two weeks. The time after his breakthrough and subsequent acceptance by Gerrit Klein and Boden Meler.
Two weeks of an ever-increasing torrent of boasting rhetoric from the two SS operatives at the Schroder piggery. Details that left Dieter Falke in great distress. Their apparent joy in

their work. The lack of any hint of understanding that they were dealing with fellow humans. More an almost childish need for praise from their superior officer as to the blind, maniacal efficiency of their undertakings. Numbers not people were their focus, processing the volumes, together with a sadistic delight in participating in the hands-on parts of the operations, such as the injecting phenol into human hearts. This latter technique had them quite animated as they described the cleverness of their subterfuge. It was their ongoing work in the slaughter of thousands of children that brought Dieter close to abandoning his mission in order to beat them both to death on the spot.

How easy it was to kill the children because they dumbly sat and obeyed the 'doctor' and only a flicker of reaction when the needle was driven into their chest.

"They just shudder and drop. It is so easy. We pick them up and toss them in the next room and in comes the next one, all ready to be dispatched."

Some laughter at this bit.

Another part of their story that greatly worried Dieter Falke was their mention of the delight they took in murdering the traitors of National Socialism. Those who would dare to speak out against the Fuhrer or question his wisdom.

For them, they designed particularly vicious ways to end their lives. Each case was considered and they devised delightful new methods to end their days in the most agony as possible.

"It was these deviants that lost us the war, Sir. It is obvious, the Fuhrer was betrayed at his moment of glory and final victory. It is why Germany suffers as it does today. We were so close to our goals."

Dieter listened and nodded in fake appreciation of their on-going tales.

Here were products of the Nazi way. How could he have fought for such an insane regime? These men were not clever, thinking adults, they were automatons. Puppets of a crazed regime that turned people into the monsters he saw before him. Briefly, he felt pity for them. Were they incapable of rational thought? Could they not step back and see how they had been manipulated? Did they really have all their humanity removed?

In the end, he decided that they were responsible, in every fibre of their bodies for their actions. Every thinking adult has choices in life. They embraced their jobs with relish. They disgusted him to a point where he would stop on the way home from each meeting and sit in the nearby woods to compose himself before continuing to his home.

As they approached the first fields of Muller orchards, Adriane took Dieter's hand.

"Look," she said. She pointed at some Linden trees silhouetted against the night sky.

"I love those trees. They remind me of the farm where I was raised. Some fond memories."

After a brief stop beneath the trees, they continued to the gates of the farm.

Hauke was not asleep. Hearing his new parents leave he immediately became concerned. Why would they go out into the night? Why would they leave him like this?

Now he was only a short distance behind them, hidden in the shadows. Watching and walking quietly.

He would go to the window at the side of the Muller's house. He would tap lightly on the window to wake Mila in her little back room. Perhaps she would know why Adriane and Dieter were here at this hour on this night. Now that they were good friends, they shared so much. They sat together in the orchards where nobody could see and talked about many things. They shared the stories of their lives. Hauke liked the way Mila would quickly look away then back with a smile. He liked her eyes, her nose, her legs. At times they held hands and once recently she kissed his cheek as they parted. Together they would solve the mystery of this late-night visiting.

Chapter 26

'The Meeting'

They met in one of the Muller's large packing sheds.
When Adriane and Dieter entered, the low-level discussions
amongst those in attendance, stopped altogether.
About twenty people were present.
Egon Kingele approached. He shook Dieter's hand and
hugged Adriane, then motioned to the small assembly.
"These are all the anti-fascist people of this area. Those of
us who survived. We're not communists or idealists just
Germans who recognised evil when they saw it."
He was speaking for the group. His voice rose.
"Dieter, I realise what you have undertaken was not a pleasant task and we greatly appreciate your commitment.
Hold no information back. It is best that we understand what
we have in our midst. As proud Germans, we have to admit
that our nation is ruined and it is divided. Perhaps there will
be nothing we can do but it is important to have the informa-

tion. To know what happened in this country during the last decade. Are you well, can you proceed?"

Dieter looked about. He saw the Mullers, the Kingeles and the Schroders. Walter and Ilse Schroder would tonight, discover the exact nature of the men they harboured. It had been agreed that Dieter would reveal nothing beforehand so as not to jeopardise any interaction between these people and their employees. He hoped they were ready.

In the background, he noted Markus and Antje Keller. There were others he did not know or recognised only as fellow citizens or farmers.

Egon appeared at his side with a tumbler of drink.

"Schnapps," he said. "It helps with public speaking."

Dieter was briefly amused.

"Thank you, Egon. Perhaps if we gather around and all be seated, I can talk softly."

There followed some rearranging of positions. Small empty barrels were dragged forward. Others found chairs. Once in a tight circle he addressed the people.

before him.

"For any who do not know, I was an Oberleutnant in the 9th Fallschirmjaeger Regiment. A Wehrmacht soldier. I fought for this country because it is my country. I did not fight for what it became.

For the purpose of speaking to the two men at the piggery, I invented a position for myself in the Schutzgruppen as a Hauptsturmführer in charge of transport. In this case, trans-porting people to our extermination camps."

There was a slight murmur in the group as if these words were still forbidden or misunderstood.

"From what I know since wars end we had many of these camps. They were for murdering people, other humans, especially Jews, on a massive scale. We cannot walk away from these actions. Pretend it was a mistake or the work of others, that we did not know, followed orders or that somehow it is all forgiven. I speak the way I feel. Anyway, I told them I knew that they were SS and that it was safe to talk to me. I revealed myself as the SS officer. Despite my considerable lack of knowledge concerning the inner working of our SS units they did not question me or seek reassurances. My act, by chance, fitted exactly into their profiles and the world they inhabited. It was as if they were waiting to meet a fellow just like me so that they could relax and tell their story. To boast most completely about their exploits, their techniques and their vile undertakings. They have no remorse, only pride. Ilse Koch, you were right. These are the two men you saw at Auschwitz. They were of minor rank but two of the ringmasters in the slaughter."

Dieter paused. The faces around him were drained of emotion. They sat in silence, their heads lowered.

"Before I proceed I must warn you that you may not want to hear what I have to tell you next. I will spare nothing. When I have finished you may feel horror, you may feel sick. I doubt any of you will be proud to call yourselves German.

Well, certainly not this group. Perhaps we will be able to take heart from the fact that a few of us do know such details and have not turned our heads. I have my own feelings about this newest information. My life, all our lives may prove simpler if we do not know. But now I must press on."

Egon, sitting next to Dieter patted his knee.

"Please continue my friend."

Early in Dieter's revelations, while he spoke of Scharfuhrer Meler's alleged cleverness at walking the participants into the anti-room before the gas chamber, he was interrupted Ilse Koch held up her hand.

"I was there," she said forcefully. "Here is the truth. These men are fools if they think for one moment that the poor wretches they herded to the gas chambers were somehow entranced by their silver-tongued speeches about showers and a glowing future.

Those chosen each time understood. They knew, they all knew. They had the name for it.

They'd say, "Oh God, it is our turn. We're going there."

'Going where?" asked Egon.

Ilse looked about the room.

"They called it …… 'The Knowing Room'. Why?

Because they knew they were about to die. We're going to 'the knowing room', they'd whisper. It was a simple blind acceptance that drove them on, to obey and walk into that dreaded chamber. There was nothing they could do. Their end had come. At the hands of Germans. Yes, us! Germans."

She threw up her arms in disgust and flopped back into her seat. Her husband comforted her as the rest of the room bowed their heads once more at the utter shame of it all.

Dieter Falke continued. It was his time to delve into details of the techniques. The methods, the madness, the hideous cruelty, the joy as the two men described the pain, torture, suffering, humiliation or the clinical precision of their work. He left no detail from his descriptions. Even as he heard gasps, then crying, he continued.

After over half an hour of most excruciating detail, he finally
stopped.

Then simply added.

"That is all I have learned to date."

For a while, the shed stayed silent. Finally, Egon stood and
held up his arms.

"My friends, citizens. We wanted to know the truth. Now we
have it. I don't think we should talk anymore tonight. It is all
too fresh and harsh. Can I suggest we adjourn for now?
Think about what we have heard. Consider it all. Let us meet
once more a week from now and talk about what, if any,
action we can or should take. Can you raise your hands if
you agree to this proposal."

Slowly all the hands in the room were raised. People stood
and quietly shuffled out into the night. Some walked, others
started vehicles and drove away. Soon the shed was empty
except for Egon and Martha Kingele and the Mullers.

Egon shook Dieter's hand once more.

"You've done all you could. Truth can be a terrible burden.
Thank you again for your support. Can I offer you transport
to your door."

Dieter looked at his neighbour, then at Adriane.

"No, we enjoyed the walk. Your truck might wake Hauke."

As he turned to leave Dieter was confronted by Klaus Muller.
His face was grave.

"Can I speak with you, outside," he said. "I need to tell you
something" He indicated to the door.

In the darkness at the side of the shed, the two men faced
each other.

Dieter could only see an outline of Klaus Muller.

"Your information in there made me realise I should consider a possibility concerning the death of my sister and her family."

"The ones killed in the British bombing raid?"

"I'm afraid that was just an invention on my part to allay any suspicion concerning Mila, suddenly living here at the farm."

"Your sister, she was involved in your network?"

"Yes. Also her husband. Our opposition was simply verbal. We were not about to undermine the German state. Still, even voicing views contrary to the total dedication to the Fuhrer was enough. Somebody betrayed them. We'll never know who. Possibly a neighbour. They were raided. My sister, husband and two children, a boy aged nine and a girl aged eight were all taken away. Mila, who was eleven then, was holidaying with us at the time so we told her the bombing story and she stayed."

The man paused and in the dark. He coughed a little.

"We made inquiries. Their movements could be traced to some extent. Somehow they were sent to Auschwitz.
It is there that any information ends."

There ensued a silence. Dieter could not see his companion's face.

"Klaus, your story is terrible of course but what are you trying to say?"

"When you described the special treatment handed down to traitors. I wondered, could the two Scharfuhrers we were discussing tonight .... could they have been the ones who murdered my sister and her family?"

Dieter felt a coldness creep over him. Of course. The man was right. There was a very real chance that they were the perpetrators.

Klaus spoke again.

"You can say no. You have done so much. If they are the monsters you describe they may not even remember a specific case. But if there is a chance of knowing how they died. It would be of great comfort."

Dieter put out his arm and guided the man back into the light at the front of the shed.

"Klaus, I'll do my best to bring it into the conversation. Can you give as much detail as possible about them? There will be a way I can bring the matter up."

Back in the darkness, under the shed where they had listened to the whole evening's proceedings, Hauke now held Mila. He hugged her tightly. He had only just taken his hand from her mouth where he had smothered her groans as they sat so close to the feet of the two men as they spoke in the darkness.

Now he held her as she cried softly. His mouth crumpled. One or two of his own tears dripped on her neck.

Chapter 27

'A Plan'

Hauke made it to his bed. He ran across the fields of their neighbours and skipped through fences that only a child would know.

After delivering Mila back through her bedroom window and agreeing to say nothing for the moment he was pleased with his efforts. He lay under his covers, trying to quell his panting as he listened to Dieter and Adriane return. He waited as they paused to look in his door and check that he was sleeping.

Once he was sure they had themselves retired for the night he slipped out of his bed, removed his clothes and climbed back under his covers.

He lay awake most of the night, afraid to sleep, afraid of the horrors playing in his head, puzzled by the stories of what people did to other people and heartbroken on behalf of Mila. They needed to talk, to go over the situation. He wanted to make plans. Anger was in his mind.

Could he be a hero for this girl? In his last heroic act back in the Berlin apartment he nearly died.

When he awoke with light in the window, it was with a start as he felt a needle pierce his chest. For a while, he lay still his eyes flicking about the room as he realised that he was safe and the dream had its origins in the previous night.

In the mid-morning Egon could be seen making his way across his field toward their house. He found Dieter at the front of his barn pouring petrol into the tank of his new motorbike.

"I thought they filled the bikes when they loaded them in the truck? I know you haven't ridden yours yet."

Dieter looked up.

"There was room for a little more. I plan to go for a ride, away from the town along some quiet rural roads while I remind myself how to ride a motorbike."

He laid his hand on the controls.

"These are well-made machines. We Germans do engineering so well. What a pity ……. "

Egon sniffed. He hitched his trousers, as was his way and flicked his bracers.

"Yes, indeed."

He walked closer to Dieter.

"You gave us all so much to think about last night. I doubt any of us were ready for the truth in all its raw detail. You're a soldier, respectfully, you may be a little more immune. Myself, I am sick. Physically sick. It is beyond my understanding that such people exist. Yet they do.

Now we must decide, what comes next. It cannot be left

alone. That much I know."

Dieter climbed onto his bike, hunching his shoulders as he reached for the handlebars. He flexed his hands over the throttle and brakes.

"It's why we need a week for all of us to absorb the information and make a decision."

He pumped the pedals tentatively then pushed down hard. The engine burst into life. He revved the machine a couple of time and then let it die down.

"First time," he said. "That's impressive."

"The Americans will hang them."

Dieter looked Egon.

"Of course they will. You cannot be concerned about that?"

"We will still have to live in this town, Dieter. People will not like us betraying, even monsters."

"That is why we must think about this for a week."

Dieter revved his bike and rolled away, leaving his neighbour standing alone, looking lost.

He felt unease at cutting the conversation short when the man was troubled and wanted to talk but he too was unsure of the future. A ride with the wind in his hair might help.

He wanted to consider what assistance he might be able to render in regard to the death of Klaus Muller's sister. Their conversation remained a secret. He did not want to trouble Adriane nor tell others. Could he be of any help at all?

He had felt his role was near to or at an end. Now it might be extended. If he asked the two murderers about a specific family they would become suspicious. Would they even remember? Their catalogue of crime was vast. He needed a diversion to introduce the subject in such a way as to allow the two a chance to be boastful once more. To take pleasure in detailing another aspect of their work. A particular circumstance.

What could it be?

A short distance from their farm he saw Hauke walking along the road toward the Muller orchards. He dropped the bike's revs and pulled up next to the boy.

"Hop on the back. I'll give you a lift."

Hauke ran his eyes over the machine. He seemed unsure not meeting Dieter's eyes.

"No thank you, I'd like to walk."

"Are you going to see Mila?"

"Yes."

"You like her a lot, don't you.?"

The boy looked a little annoyed at being questioned about such delicate matters.

"Yes, I do."

"Last chance for a ride on our new bike."

"Perhaps another day."

Dieter accelerated away. He was quite hurt. His son had refused to ride with him. He wanted to feel the boy's arms around his waist, holding on to his father, reassured and safe. To be close to this young fellow who he realised had shared so much of his recent life.

He could tell when Hauke was unhappy. Right now he seemed a little lost in thought. Was it just his liking for the girl? Perhaps that was all. Such feelings would be new to him. He would find a quiet moment to speak to him in a way that a father should. His time with his own father would serve as a model for his methods. He felt they were sound.

At the Muller farm, Hauke avoided the family and crept to
the back of one of their outer sheds.
Mila sat on the grass in the shadow of the building's roof.
She stood as she saw the boy approach. They hugged briefly.
She smoothed down her dress.
"Let's go," she said.
Below the edge of a field, through the rows of apple trees,
they made their way to the road and then, after checking,
crossed and ran into the copse of pine trees opposite one
end of the property.
There, at last alone, unseen, they sat down cross-legged on
the spongy pine needle forest floor. They faced each other.
Her dress was linen with small blue flowers circling the hem.
Hauke spoke first.
"What do we do?"
He reached out and took her hand, staring with purpose into
her eyes.

Chapter 28

'Farm Life'

They all drove into the town. It was quite an event. The first time that all three were together in their new truck. Adriane needed to see the doctor. The time was moving closer when there would be a fourth in their household. Perhaps wary of gossip, Dieter parked the truck in an open area behind the main street rather than in the square. The man who moved into that farm, now had a new truck? What next?
The doctor was senior. Too old to have done anything but seen out the war by staying put in his practice. They sat and waited. The only patients in the cosy room until a young woman entered, bid them Guten Tag and went into the doctor's rooms.
When they entered, the doctor introduced the woman as an American Army doctor. To help me a little he explained and gain some local knowledge of medical practices.
The woman spoke excellent German and took Adriane aside

179

for a thorough check. The doctor used the time to have Hauke lay down on his bench and pressed the boy's stomach asking if there was any discomfort. His interest in Hauke followed his initial examination of the boy when he first arrived in Willingen.

'All seems fine," he said.

He repeated a phrase he had used before.

"Who would have thought. Good Russian doctors."

Dieter liked the man. He was cautious, thorough and despite his reserve, there was an underlying kindness.

He wore a waistcoat and fob watch. The watch utilised when checking pulse or blood pressure.

"It is a quiet day," he said. "In a way, that is good. No sick people, a healthy town."

"Oh, don't worry. I'm sure there will be a small epidemic soon to keep you occupied."

The man enjoyed Dieter's joke and laughed.

It was doubtful he was a fascist. More likely a careful man who kept his own counsel. Neutrality was a safe position for his profession.

"Is the American doctor to be a permanent member of your practice?" Dieter asked.

"Unfortunately not. The Americans realised that there was a serious shortage of doctors in Hesse so they have been lending out their own personnel to help out. It will be reviewed every two months."

Adriane emerged from the anti-room with the American doctor.

"All is well," the doctor said quite brightly. "Adriane is entering the final semester so you two men will need to be attentive and also ready should the child decide to make an early entry into the world."

She shook Adriane's hand.

"Till next time. I should still be in this area. I have seen your local hospital. It is quite good. All will be well."

Their German doctor nodded in agreement and showed them out.

There were three people in the waiting room.

"Perhaps the epidemic has begun."

He winked at Dieter.

They walked through the main street to the store where Markus Keller worked. Dieter was hoping they might have some bolt cutters he could afford. Cutting off nails protruding from old pieces of wood would be a lot quicker than his current method of driving them out with a hammer.

Markus smiled at the request.

"Who uses bolt cutters? I have a big drum full of them from army stores. You can probably afford a large pair and a small pair."

He was right.

In their conversation, Dieter casually asked, "Markus, I know you were in the Wehrmacht. What did you do? You've never mentioned it."

Markus Keller leaned over the counter. He took a breath.

"I was a Scharfschütze. It is not something the Americans and the British like to hear, so I don't talk about it much. Neither of them likes snipers. Actually, nobody does. Not playing by the rules I guess. Sneaky. Nasty people. I'm not proud. It was a job."

Dieter touched the man's shoulder. Tugged his apron strap in odd solidarity.

"Then no more will be said, my friend."

With some spare funds from the sale of corn and potatoes, the trio next went to a secondhand clothing shop. They found some shorts and two shirts for Hauke, a rather full dress that would fit Adriane in her state and Dieter fitted himself with two pair of quite sturdy work pants. Men's shirts and boots could not be found. He would have to repair his current ones.

They bought store bread and some jam. After they paid the lady in the shop asked them to wait. She disappeared through a curtain to her residence at the back. They could hear her bustling about. When she returned she held a bundle of baby clothes and handed them to Adriane.
"For you," she said. "To start you off. My children are grown. I've waited for somebody like you to come into my shop. It is time to pass them on. I hope all is well for you. If your next child is as handsome as your son then you will be pleased."
Dieter noticed Hauke enjoy the moment.
The lady had not taken into account Adriane's age and the impossibility of her statement. Still, it was a nice moment. Somebody cared.

As they turned a corner to return to their truck a man almost bumped into them. He took a step back.
"Entshuldegen," he said. Then looking up they realised he was a face from their meeting at the Muller's shed. A dapper man in a waistcoat and alpine hat. He appeared about to speak then looked at Hauke and smiled, tipped his hat and stepped down onto the gutter to move past.

Adriane exchanged glances with Dieter.

As they approached their truck they saw Hans Koch walking across the corner of the area in the distance.
He looked up and waved a greeting. At the same moment, Boden Meler came round the corner bringing the two men face to face. They stopped momentarily on the narrow foot-path while Boden Meler looked round to see who the post office man was acknowledging. His eyes rested on Dieter. Briefly, his hand moved to also wave then dropped. He turned away with his head down and hurried on. Hans Koch looked their way then continued his walk.
The threesome had stopped.
Dieter Falke looked at the space where the confrontation took place.
A word came into his head.
"Stuttgart," he thought.

Chapter 29

'Foundations'

As he entered the Schroder property Dieter noted that the poles were being placed for the foundations of the new building.

Walter Schroder was with his two employees supervising their work. He was checking alignment and levels with a string line.

As Dieter's motorbike caught their attention Walter walked up the slope to the main yard well away from the men.

He dusted some dirt from his pants and stamped his feet to clear some clods of dirt from his boots.

"The soil is very solid down there. Hard digging the holes. They complain all the time. I have a great deal of trouble holding my tongue. Sometimes I look at one or the other and wonder if they note the hatred in my eyes."

Dieter parked his bike.

"Everybody appreciates what you're having to endure

Walter. None more so than me. Hopefully, a resolution will be forthcoming."

The man shrugged.

"What can I do. It's a situation."

He looked at Dieter's bike.

"You usually come by in your truck?"

"I thought this would be more dramatic. Let's point at your building site shall we. I am supposed to be guiding you with my architectural expertise."

Walter duly waved his arms in the direction of the work.

"I wasn't expecting you again. I thought you had gathered all the information we sought."

Dieter looked at the man. He did not wish to disclose Klaus Muller's confidence.

"I also thought that was the case but something else has been nagging me. I'd rather not say until I'm sure. Can we create some minor problem that will require a stop work? I'll wait till these two are settled somewhere then approach to do some measurements or something and instigate another conversation."

The morning progressed. The men continued to dig. Their efforts appearing lazy and truculent. They cursed the clay soil and abused their implements as they knocked clods of earth from the blades.

After a suitable time, Dieter and Walter appeared and at a distance began a small charade as if discussing an issue regarding the work.

Walter then retreated to his house while Dieter strolled down to the worksite.

"Hullo again," he said casually.

"You can take a rest, my friends."

Boden Meler and Gerrit Klein leaned on their shovels. Their entitled air was still apparent.

"What is it now?"

Dieter waved his hand in what he hoped was a superior and dismissive attitude.

"Herr Schroder has not allowed properly for drainage."

While patently untrue Dieter relied on a lack of building fundamentals on the part of his two companions to bypass the point.

"We thought so too," said Gerrit. "The way the man carries himself about this site you would think he is the expert rather than you."

Dieter sat down on a grassy slope next to the diggings.

"Ah well, it is his building. He should take an interest. It will be easy enough to fix. Here sit down while I look things over."

The men sat on the grass while Dieter wandered about looking over the edge of the slope and making notes.

He then returned to the two men.

"Yes, not really a problem. Though it will require a little extra digging."

The men groaned and he laughed at their misery. One slapped his knee and shook his head.

"Your visits provide a little relief," said Boden.

Dieter waited, then just nodded.

He paused again and produced his officer's stare. Fixing his look until two men were suitably unnerved.

"You know, this is an opportune moment. Something has intrigued me. I may as well ask. Considering the coincidences in our meeting to date it is worth pursuing."

He waited once more, enjoying the control.

"What is it?" they asked in unison. Their eagerness was palpable.

"Alright. Call this a whimsical question. I doubt you will have the answer. Your memories would have to be exceptional. Let me try ...... I am from Stuttgart. I lived with my wife on Neckartrasse, in an apartment building. It was a very pleasant place, close to the centre of the city and to the Unterer Schlossgarten. Just after I left to go on permanent duty my wife wrote to me with great glee to inform me that the Gestapo had taken away a family from our building. They were a loathsome group of four. They had two children, I had thought three but she saw only two taken out on the day. We had disliked them for some time. Always voicing doubts and opinions about our Fuhrer and the glories of National Socialism. Anyway, they must have said or done something that tipped off the Gestapo. Perhaps some decent citizen reported them, having had enough. Either way, they were removed."

Dieter paused again. The two men were intent on his every word. Anxious to please.

"Now, here is the interesting part. It occurred to me the other day when I saw you Boden in the town, that they may well have been despatched to Auschwitz. I do not recall them coming through my area but keep in mind we were handling many thousands. I would not have been aware of individuals. It would give me great pleasure to know that you took care of these enemies of the Reich and I would be fascinated to hear of your methods."

Dieter spread his hands like a friendly uncle.

Both men, he could tell were ready to pounce on this opportunity to shine.

"What were their names?"

"I don't know individually but the family name was Breitbarth. I'll fully understand if you cannot recall …….."

It was as if a large light had been lit in the eyes of the two men opposite.

"Ah, ah, yes, yes," they cried.

They slapped each other in unison, smiling and laughing.

"Of course. It is the unusual name," said Gerrit Klein.

"Breitbarth. It means big beard or something. That and the fact that they were not at all repentant. Nearly all who came to us for crimes against the Reich were humble, hoping to earn a reprieve, grovelling before us. Some did, for a while. Earn some time."

Boden Meler cut in.

"Perhaps they thought they were just to be locked up and nothing more. The father kept on denouncing the war effort. He called the Fuhrer insane and predicted our downfall. He spoke loudly and often. When we warned him to shut-up …… and this is why we remember, he called us fools and lackeys of the state, too stupid to realise we had been duped. By this stage, others were taking note. It could not go on. Having prisoners being openly defiant. So we planned a fitting end to his escapades. Something that would make others think twice."

Dieter swallowed. He did his best to appear pleased and eager to hear the details while dreading what was to come.

It was Gerrit Klein who began, rubbing his hands together as he spoke. He told of how on a sunny morning they took the two Breitbarth parents to their injecting room. Both were tied to posts in a darkened corner. They were tied tightly and gagged. They faced the brightly lit injecting area. Even then the man was defiant trying to talk. Only when their children were brought in did they cease struggling. Perhaps they realised too late that their actions had brought this upon them. The two children were stripped down. There was no pretence of a doctor or examination this time. They were held with the arms pinned back and turned to face their parents. Then as the parents watched Boden and Klein each drove the phenol injection syringes very slowly into the children's chests. The bodies were held in full view of the parents while they shuddered and died.

After that the parents were untied and dragged to the next room where their children's bodies lay. Boden seemed so pleased with their narrative that he apologised for the final information.

Having had their fun they simply shot both parents in the back of the head and let them fall with their children. Then they left and celebrated with a beer.

"I tell you what," he concluded. "It worked. When we tied them up and took away their children and then shot them. Haha. They didn't say another word."

Dieter looked at the two men for some time. He couldn't speak. They, in turn, looked a little uneasy. He had to react.

"Brilliant," he said at last. "Absolutely brilliant. You're right of course. That would have held their tongues. I am most pleased with this information. What a wonderful day."

He rose and tapped both men's shoulders. They looked like two children praised for their schoolwork.

As he turned to go he asked another question.

"How did you come to be in Willingen? It is not an obvious place to be. Which is the point I assume."

Both men laughed.

"With the Russians approaching us in Poland we decided it would be best to be gone. It would not be wise to return to our homes. Then we remembered a wonderful time we both had when we were in the Hitler Youth. There was a month-long camp right here in Willingen. We remembered it fondly. Who would think to look for us here."

Dieter smiled.

"Of course. Clever."

As he made to walk away Gerrit asked, "So you are from Stuttgart. Why are you here?"

Off guard, Dieter hesitated then turned back to the man.

"I think you two just answered that question. I once stopped here years ago. I had a pleasant meal and got drunk with some farmers. The idea stuck in my mind. I could not return to Stuttgart for safety's sake. Also my apartment and my wife did not survive the war. Let me say I acquired some wealth during the last days of our conflict. So I took a new wife, came to Willingen and bought a farm."

Gerrit smirked.

"Acquired some money. Of course." Then he added, "Who is the boy?"

"An orphan. The son of a dear colleague. It is not something I talk about."

Suitably chastened the men stepped back and seemed as if they were about to salute. They stopped themselves.

As Dieter walked back to his motorbike he considered his

ability to ad-lib his story. His main concern was the story he was obliged to relate to Klaus Muller.

Chapter 30

'Decisions'

Alone on a chair at the front of the small crowd, Klaus Muller appeared removed by his thoughts to some dark place.
His head bowed he took little interest in the conversations around him, his eyes focused intently on the floor of his shed. Normally a confident, neatly dressed man, he seemed indifferent to his appearance. Several days unshaven and wearing rough work clothes and boots he sat unmoving not even acknowledging greetings from his neighbours.
There were more people this time. Near double the previous meeting. The buzz of their conversation was low key as if guarding opinions had priority.
Seated next to Klaus and his wife were Adriane, Dieter and the Kingeles.
The shed had filled quickly at the appointed time. It could only be assumed that they were all involved and interested in the case. There was no way of knowing the loyalties of

all. Since the war's end stories changed and secrets became embedded in the narrative. Even in a small town, nothing was certain.

Dieter rose and the people quickly fell silent. He felt isolated. Adriane squeezed his hand and he smiled down at her on the chair beside him. Soon to be the mother of their child.

He cleared his throat before speaking.

"Thank you all for coming. Your support is most appreciated. I am at a loss where to begin. Please be patient with my message and let me tell it all. As some of you know I have been using subterfuge to garner information from the two men who are employed at the Schroder family farm. Acting in the role of a fictitious former SS commander.

It has been quite demanding. I am able to report that nobody has broken our silence on the matter and so the two men remain unaware of my real reasons for speaking to them."

"Do you have any more information for us?" A voice asked from the crowd.

Dieter wondered whether the questioner was a supporter of their quest or a supporter of the two men and their actions. He looked across at Klaus. The man raised his head, his face torn by his misery. He nodded to Dieter.

"Yes," said Dieter. "I have some further knowledge of the operations of these two men. It is of a very personal nature and has caused great shock and sadness for one of us here tonight. After some discussion with Klaus he decided that I should share this story with you. I feel it may make our course of action plainer once you hear the details. I have been told to leave nothing out."

It took only the first few sentences from Dieter's story for the

crowd to become silent. As it progressed they bowed their heads. Here was the raw truth of sadism on display and this time they could relate the events to one of their own.
A family many had met at times when they visited from Stuttgart. A girl in their midst who would have suffered the same fate had she been at home the day they were taken away.
The story of the family's death in a bombing raid was false. Not some unknown people in another country. Not some Jewish citizens from the cities whom they did not understand. This was real and close.
Many wept. It was a new level of personal horror. German on German. A type of fanatical hatred that was prevalent in the cities but vague and unspoken in small towns.

Dieter included the manner in which he was told of their fate. Not a shame-filled whisper. A guilt-ridden, wringing of hands admission. No, a bravado-filled, boastful exercise with both participants talking over each other in order to ensure every detail was faithfully reproduced. It was their utter enthusiasm and lust that he hoped he conveyed with certainty.

He waited when finished. It was a method he was becoming familiar in using. Quite a few members of the crowd stepped forward to lay hands on Klaus Muller and offer words of comfort.

When he resumed Dieter could not help but search the faces of the crowd for any signs of dissent. Some who might interrupt their solidarity by concluding that Melor and Klein were somehow heroes of the state.

"If we are to move forward in our post-war country then I feel we need first to take care of the past. If we don't it will always be there like some unwelcome house guest. Reminding us by its presence that it is still to be cast out.

Can I, therefore, suggest some options for your consideration. If any of you have other suggestions please make them known.

1. We do nothing.

2. We confront these two murderers and force them to leave this town.

3. We contact the Americans and tell them all we know.

Hauke was not at home when Adriane and Dieter returned. His luck held as they looked in on his darkened room. A carefully arranged pair of pillows made up for his missing figure.

"He sleeps so quietly," smiled Adriane.

"He'll snore in his old age," Dieter whispered.

They went downstairs to sit and to talk about the night. Discussions with the crowd took over an hour. Despite the terrible news they now all shared, the feeling was one of mistrust of the Americans.

Unanimously it seemed they all felt punishment, even hanging, was appropriate but they were reluctant to hand two countrymen over to the enemy. Even an enemy that seemed quite decent.

It was agreed that the local German police could do nothing and just asking the two to leave was too weak as a response. Following orders was mentioned as an excuse for their actions but this was quickly dismissed on the grounds of human decency with Hans and Lena Koch reminding all about of how close they had come to a similar fate. Which would probably have been carried out by these very men or similar SS operatives.

Other thoughts and ideas came and went. Some angry, some absurd but all given a hearing.

One man suggested that they were all missing a course of action that satisfied all their standards for punishment. When asked what that action might be he confessed he did not know. He felt they simply had not thought of it yet. Finally, it was Klaus Muller who rose to his feet and in doing so, silenced the room. The crowd looked at him in a combination of respect and curiosity.

"This news," he said, has torn away part of my soul. I am aware that virtually everybody in Germany has been touched by this war. A war that we created. I loved my sister and her family most deeply. Their arrest and disappearance affected me deeply. After all this time you know I still held a belief that somehow they had survived and we would see them again. It was a forlorn hope I agree. The next best thought that I could consider was that they died peacefully and quickly. A merciful death gave me a little comfort. For Mila's sake, I created the story of the bombing of their apartment.

Now I find that their execution was conducted in a most vile and heinous manner aimed at inflicting the most pain, suffering and misery. To find it fitting to have two parents forced to watch their dear children being slowly, hideously murdered …… Looking into their eyes …. "

The man sat down once more, as if all his strength had ebbed away.

"Whatever fate you decide for these two men. It will not be enough to satisfy my needs."

At this moment, as the crowd stood in silence, unable to make headway, the Muller's six-year-old son Lambert appeared at the edge of the crowd.

They parted, as if he were a celestial vision. Ursula Muller rushed to the boy.

"Have you been here long?"

"No," he said, "I could not sleep. Why are all these people here?"

The boy's appearance galvanised the assembly. Perhaps they looked at the small body in his nightshirt and transferred their thoughts to the murdered family.

A vote was taken. It seemed unanimous. Dieter, together with Egon Kingele and Walter Schroder would document every piece of information they could muster about the two Auschwitz operatives and it would be duly presented to the American senior staff. Then wheels would be set in motion. Justice would be served and the people could close that chapter of their lives. They were not betraying these men. They were not fit to be called Germans.

Hauke moved as quietly as possible through their cornfield. The husks brushed his shoulder and made what seemed to be an excessive amount of noise.

His bed made up of pillows must have worked, otherwise, his 'parents' would be out looking for him.

Now clear of the field, he crept toward the house. A light was on in the main room. If he could get inside through the back door then he may be able to ascend the stairs without being noticed. Avoiding the fourth step that always squeaked.

It had taken nearly a great amount of time after the crowd

left the Muller's farm for Hauke to feel he could leave Mila alone.

Taking the same position under the floor of the apple shed they had sat in the darkness during the first meeting, they expected to hear a decision as to what action may be taken regarding the two SS men at Schroder's piggery.

Mila sensed there may be an escalation to their story.

Her uncle Klaus had barely spoken for days. Occasionally he would find her and give her long hugs, kissing the top of her head, muttering, "Dear Mila." Then head down once more he would walk away aimless and distracted.

At first, Dieter's words seemed general in nature. Then as he progressed the crowd grew especially quiet and they were able to hear all the details as he spoke. Once Hauke realised what was being said he reached out to Mila in the dark.

He felt her arm and then her face. They were wet. This news was so horrifying the girl was beyond screaming or crying out. She just shook. Hauke held onto her and cradled her head. He felt helpless. Then he became aware of the emotions welling up in his own body. Despite all his world-weary experience in misery and suffering, he was crushed by this new revelation. It seemed the world could sink to newer more terrible depths.

He managed to take the girl back to her room. Climbing in the window behind her he made her remove her shoes and crawl under the covers.

"We need time to think, dear Mila. Your Uncle Klaus will want to tell you eventually but he has enough grief right now. His happiness is that you do not know."

This seemed to strike home. The girl quietened.

Hauke waited, wiping his eyes, trying to settle himself and be strong.

Mila lifted her head slightly from the pillow. Her shaking and crying stopped. Her face was just visible in the dim light.

She reached out and ran her hand across Hauke's cheek. Her eyes were strange. She half-smiled. Then she squeezed her eyes shut and began to shake once more.

Hauke sat beside her bed. He held her hand crushed against her chest beneath the blankets.

At one stage a light came on in the hallway. He ducked down as the door opened briefly. Ursula Muller held her boy Lambert's small hand. She stood for some seconds looking in at the girl's resting form then the door closed once more,

Hauke remained cramped next to the bed. He was afraid to move his hand. He prayed that Mila had fallen asleep but when eventually he did try to drag his hand away she held it tighter.

A minute or so later, strangely calm, she sat up and put her arms around Hauke's neck. She gave a long shuddering intake of breath as she held him. She kissed his cheek.

This new calm alarmed the boy even more.

"Will you be alright?" he asked.

At first, she said nothing, then she retreated and lay back on her pillow.

"Yes, I will be alright. You should go now. Please don't worry about me. Everything will be alright."

She reached out and touched his cheek once more.

"You are a lovely person Hauke Falke."

Chapter 31

'Planning'

Dieter sat at their kitchen table with Egon. Both had coffee and some home-made biscuits. Each had a writing pad and a pencil. A number of sheets were already covered with their notes.

Lena Koch would type their finished proclamations into legible sheets ready for presentation to the Americans.

Hauke descended the stairs. He wore just his shorts. Too tired and unable to find anything else when he crept unseen to his room in the night. An explanation he could not use.

"Does the boy not own any night attire?" asked Egon.

Dieter looked up.

"Yes he does but he seems to like a minimum of clothing."

Egon held out his arms.

"You've slept late my boy. Come, give me a hug."

Hauke obliged laying his head on the old man's shoulder.

His neighbour had become a surrogate grandfather. A role

they both enjoyed. Hauke loved him and his gruff ways.

"Get yourself some breakfast. You are too slim for my liking. Farm boys should have muscles and broad shoulders."

"And a tummy?"

Egon raised his hand in mock annoyance.

"Well, start with the tummy. It took much eating to grow mine."

As Hauke moved away to find bread and some milk Egon whispered.

"You are a lucky man to have such a child. He is kind and wise."

"I know," said Dieter. "You tell me often and you are right."

"Though, of late, he seems distant. Concerned. He should be happier."

Hauke decided not to return to the table. He would be expected to ask what the two men were doing. It would be a natural thing for him to do. Then there would be a vague explanation and he would be dismissed anyway.

As he moved outside to sit on a chair in the sun Walter Schroder bustled in the doorway. He patted the boy on the head.

"Morgen, Hauke Falke. Has someone stolen your clothes?"

They looked into each other's eyes and smiled.

Hauke took up a position facing the morning light.

He closed his eyes and leaned back in the solid wooden chair resting his toasted bread on his stomach. His eyes closed. He sipped his warm drink then relaxed.

The outward appearance of calm denied the turmoil in the boy's mind.

His thoughts continued to focus on his night with Mila and

their odd parting. He wanted to run across the fields to their farm right now. Call her name and have her greet him with at least a semblance of peace.

It would be too obvious. Adults would become suspicious. Questions would be asked. Perhaps it could be passed off as some childish infatuation or better still just friendship? But he did not feel he could take the chance. Beneath the quiet facade of the sunny morning, twinkling dew and silence, he knew that hearts were broken, anger boiled and a carefully considered retribution was being prepared.

He continued to sit enjoying the warmth on his body. Then, in time, became too hot. He rose, brushed the crumbs from his chest and walked back into the house.

Adriane was preparing potatoes at the sink. He watched her until she turned and gave him a hug. It was a small ritual he carried out. A quest for reassurance. He was sure nobody noticed but they did.

Passing the three men at their table he casually asked what they were doing?

"Farm production," said Egon.

"For the coming season," added Dieter.

"You've never done that before."

Walter Schroder looked up from the sheets of paper on the table.

"Well, it's more efficient to work together Hauke. You understand. A joint effort."

He gave a weak smile.

Feeling that he had shown enough interest without overplaying his role Hauke made a non-committal noise of feigned disinterest and moved on. The men at the table were absorbed in their work. He was outside their immediate thoughts.

Back in his room, he lay on his bed watching the light on the ceiling. Briefly, he thought of the apartment in Berlin with its gold ornamentation, then the white ceiling of the hospital. Both now part of his history.

His mind continued to loop back to Mila and the terrible news they had both overheard positioned under the Muller's packing shed. His parents had also died but quickly in the explosion of a bomb dropped by either British or American planes in a raid over Berlin. To hear of the deliberate, calculated, hideous cruelty inflicted on her parents by fellow Germans was an all too different matter.

With no reason other than agitation he sat up then stood and searched out some clothes. Shorts that were possibly army surplus and a blue shirt. Seated on his bed he pulled on socks and laced up his boots. He stared at the floor and sighed.

For a while, he sat on the bed unable to bring to mind a plausible excuse to walk to the Muller's farm. If he had not been privy to the story of the girl's parents it may have been easy but because he knew what was really happening downstairs and how tense the situation must be, he could not move.

The next time he became aware of his surroundings he was looking into Adriane's face. She was leaning over him touching his forehead, brushing his hair back. He blinked.

"Hullo, sleepy boy. Do you want some lunch?"

She stared into the boy's golden eyes. It had been those eyes that haunted her most when she thought of him after their parting in Berlin. She still marvelled at the fact they were united once more.

"I didn't know I'd fallen asleep again."

"That's the way sleep works. Why are you so tired?"

Hauke sensed further questioning.

"What's for lunch? Potato and ham sandwiches? Yes?"

"Well yes. I made some for the men. Come and eat with me outside. Leave the men to their work."

They sat in the shadowed entrance to their barn. Adriane had obtained a small round wrought-iron table and four matching chairs some time back. Painted dark green they were a favourite for quiet family lunches in the yard. Under a tree in the orchard or on a warm day in the shade as they were today.

When quizzed about their sudden appearance Adriane admitted that she saw them and bought them from a dealer in town. The man agreed to drop them off while Dieter was away.

Despite their lack of money at the time, Dieter said nothing as soon as he could see that his wife needed something she could claim as her own and her own enterprise.

For a while, neither attendee at their luncheon spoke. They ate the sandwiches and drank cool water with some lemon juiced squeezed in to add a little tang. Then Adriane sat straight up on her chair.

"Ooo," she said.

Hauke looked concerned.

"What? What happened."

Adriane smiled at him.

"The baby. Come, come here."

She placed the boy's hand on her distended abdomen.

"Wait. Be patient."

They waited. Then the boy lifted his hand, startled. He put it back.

"I felt it," he said. "I felt it."

"That's your new baby brother or sister. They want to come out and meet you. They will be so lucky to have a wonderful brother like you."

Hauke took his hand away. He stood for a moment looking at the ground.

Adriane took his hand.

"The answer is yes."

Hauke looked puzzled.

"What was the question?"

"What you were thinking. I have known you for a while, Hauke. I know how you think. That you are sometimes still afraid and unsure. You are my son now. I love you more than you can imagine. When the baby arrives I will love the new member of our family also but you and I Hauke we have a history. Nothing can replace what we've been through. It holds us together. We were meant to be here and that's the way it will remain. Please give me a long hug and never ever have doubts again."

After a long embrace, the boy stepped back.

"Egon gives me hugs but Dieter doesn't."

Adriane shook her head.

"Dieter is a man. He was a soldier and saw many bad things. Forgive him if he doesn't show his feelings. I've seen him watching you. You need have no doubts.

Now Egon lost his two sons in the war. I think we are his new family and you Hauke are the grandson he could never have. How much love do you want?"

The boy resumed his seat. He sat for a moment with his head down then turned and smiled.

"As much as I can get?"

They lapsed into a lengthy silence, then Adriane asked, "Hauke, what is the time? Can you look at the kitchen clock." On his return, the boy flopped back on his chair. "It's twelve minutes past one o'clock. There's somebody coming across Egon's field."

They waited, watching the edge of the rise where their field dropped away to eventually join Egon Kingele's fenceline near the bottom of the slope.

The top of a head appeared, then a forehead and slowly a face. Hauke was first to make out the figure. "It's Herr Muller," he said. "What can he want, I wonder? Perhaps he needs to see how the men are going inside." Hauke watched the man struggling onto their level ground and making his way across. He had been running. He was sweating and looked weary. Adriane waved then said, "Hauke give Herr Muller your seat." Standing, watching Hauke was concerned. Only bad news seemed to come from the Muller's farm.

Chapter 32

'Alert'

He began with an apology.
"I'm sorry to trouble you. It is concern over nothing I'm sure."
He looked at Hauke.
"Is Mila here? You and she have not seen each other for some days now, so she must have called to see you. That is so, is it not?"
The man seemed to be pleading. He was looking about as if expecting the girl to appear. Perhaps carrying a tray from the kitchen with some drinks.
Adriane answered.
"No Klaus, she is not here. Hauke?"
On cue the boy confirmed.
"No sir, Mila is not here. I have not seen her."
"Ah, then I think perhaps she has gone to walk in the woods opposite. She likes it there. It is just that she has not yet

come home for her lunch and Ursula told her she is baking dumplings. They are one of her favourites.

The threesome stood in silence. Birds cried overhead. Distantly a cow called to a calf. Then Klaus spoke again as if further explanation were needed.

"It's just that, well with the recent news I have become very aware of the girl. She is usually reliable."

He glanced at Hauke. Had he said too much?

"You have not spoken to Mila then, about .....?" asked Adriane.

"How could I? Will I ever tell her? I'm not sure."

Once again he ran his eyes over the boy standing beside them.

The atmosphere was perplexing. Hauke knew it would be better for these two people if he moved away to give the freedom to talk. His concern for Mila held him to the spot. Could she be crying in the woods? Alone?

The situation was relieved by the three men from inside the house emerging from the house doorway all talking softly.

From their deep conversation, Dieter noticed Klaus sitting in the chair and called.

"Klaus. Hullo."

As the men approached Hauke moved. He faded away. None noticed him sidle to the left and slide quietly round the side of the barn.

Klaus explained that Mila was not about the farm and not visiting here. He was concerned although he felt he had no reason to be alarmed.

The men brought chairs out from the house and sat in a circle in the shade. With the boy gone they could talk freely.

Dieter, Egon and Walter took turns in explaining the document they had hand-written. They were satisfied they had covered all the information and evidence they could muster. It was laid out in a logical manner. By working chronologically they brought the two Scharfuhrers into the scope of the death camps and then explained how they enthusiastically embraced all aspects of the most horrific executions and mass murders. It was their total dedication to their work and their desire to inflict maximum suffering and pain that they emphasised. Their search for and use of even more brutal forms of torture and death made them unfit to be called Germans and unwanted in post-war Germany.

Markus Keller would be calling by very soon to pick up their papers and transport them all to Lena Koch who would begin typing the information neatly. When finished they would all three present themselves at the nearby US Army base and ask to see the Commander. They would hand over their dossier and ask that he read the contents and take whatever action he deemed necessary.

Their task would be complete. It would be up to the Americans. If they did nothing after a week, Walter Schroder had decided he would cancel the men's employment and ask them to leave. He did not wish to have them near his home or his life any longer. It was, he pointed out, a great strain to maintain his civility whilst in their presence.

Klaus Muller seemed to be only partly aware of the information being offered. They thought he would be immensely pleased and enthusiastic about the plans but he was distracted, constantly looking way from the men talking to him. "What is it Klaus?" asked Dieter.

"I'm sorry gentlemen. Naturally, my passionate hatred of these murderers goes without saying but my mind wanders. Something tells me all is not right. Mila and Hauke are great friends. I was sure, when she was missing, that she had decided to call over here to see Hauke. She is not here and the boy seems rather vague about the whole affair. Am I missing something?"
Dieter turned to Adriane.
"Was he vague?"
"He simply said she was not here. Now I think upon it, why did he not ask more questions about his friend? Have they had a disagreement? It could be that they are simply not talking at the moment. Although they are both such forgiving children, I would find such an event hard to understand."
Klaus seemed to like this theory.
"A disagreement. That could be it. They're both sulking over some minor matter."

Their musing was interrupted by the sound of a motorbike turning into the farm from the road. They all turned to watch.
Markus Keller rode his old machine slowly up to the yard and seeing the group by the barn he switched off the engine and pushed it over onto its stand.
As he walked toward the group they noted his grave visage.
"What is it, Markus? You look concerned."
"Dieter, I am very concerned. As I came along this road I noticed the car of August Schafer parked, almost hidden, in that little copse near Walter's farm."
He lifted his finger as would a teacher.

"As somebody who is not from this area, you would be unfamiliar with August Schafer. He was and probably still is this town's most avid admirer of Hitler and all that the National Socialists represented. Since war's end, he has been discreet, keeping to himself but nobody who knows him would doubt his ongoing loyalty to the sickness that pervaded this country."

Walter Schroder spoke.

"Do you think he could possibly be at my farm? Could he be speaking to Klein and Meler?"

"I cannot see why his vehicle would be where it is for any other reason. The woods are small. My God you can't even find mushrooms there. It is a short walk to the side of the road where your new building is taking place."

"How could he have known?" asked Adriane.

"Loose talk. Perhaps not everybody at our meeting the other night was totally convinced of the validity of our actions. There are ways he could have been informed."

Dieter rubbed his chin.

"If he has spoken to them, then what might be their course of action? They would be concerned for their safety. What do such men do when in a panic? Would they move on quickly? Would this man offer them some sanctuary or a way to disappear?"

He turned to Walter Schroder.

"Most of all I'm concerned for your family, Walter. These men could be violent if they feel they are cornered and have been betrayed."

Walter Schroder's face was white. He stood, his frame shaking.

"I must get back there. There are too many omens. I need to

assure myself. Set things right. Will you help me?”

In a continuation of rapid, escalating events there came a noise at this moment from across the yard.

This time it was a woman stumbling out of the field from the same direction that had brought Klaus Muller to their presence some time before.

Ursula Muller was distressed. She ran as best she could toward them. Her husband jumped forward to meet her and helped her to a chair. She sat gasping for breath, her hands clammy, her face pale. Finally, she spoke. Adriane gave her a glass of water to sip. She spoke hoarsely.

“Please, please tell me you have found Mila.”

She looked about expectantly at the faces that surrounded her. Her eyes where wild.

“Please …. is she here?”

“No my dear.” Klaus patted his wife’s hand. “She does not appear to be here. What is wrong? Why have you run? What is troubling you?”

Ursula Muller raised her hands toward her husband wringing the air in despair.

“Your shotgun has gone Klaus. I fear Mila has taken your shotgun.”

The group conversation quickly reached a turmoil. Could the girl be depressed? Could she be in the woods at this very moment contemplating something terrible? Had the loss of her parents and siblings in what she believed to have been a bombing raid caught up with her right at a time when these adults had discovered the terrible details of their real demise?

As the discussions became more animated and urgent they all became aware of the boy Hauke standing quietly beside them. He had reappeared without anybody noticing him. His head was bowed and his face was pale. He appeared ill. They all stopped looking at his slumped shoulders His hands were locked together.

"I have something to tell you," he said.

Chapter 33

'Truth'

The boy's words left them all speechless as they contemplated the consequences.
His news of listening in on the meetings and hearing all the awful tales of atrocity was not one that they interrupted or interrogated.
When he finished they simply stood, each trying to comprehend the possibilities of such a situation.
It was his final description of the girl's reaction, her misery, her state of mind that worried them the most.
As Hauke stood in the middle of their circle, forlorn, crestfallen it was Dieter who stepped forward and took him and held his face to his chest.
"Thank you, Hauke. Thank you for telling us. Nobody here has anything but admiration for you and how you cared for Mila."
He held the boy's head in his hands turning his face up to

look into his eyes.

"You know Mila better than any of us. What does this mean?
There are two directions we could go. Which one is right?
Is she in the woods crying and thinking dark thoughts or is
she on her way to Herr Schroder's farm to confront her par-
ent's killers? Can you think carefully Hauke. If you care for
Mila, help us, tell us what to do."

Hauke stared straight back into Dieter's eyes but his focus
was elsewhere. Somewhere in his mind, he struggled with
the enormous task that had been presented to him.

One decision would be right. One would not.

The building site on the boundary was deserted. They
looked across the fields to the Schroder's shed and buildings.

Klaus wanted to go straight back to his home to ensure his
wife and son were safe and to confront the two men. He was
persuaded that this might inflame the situation. They need
to plan their approach.

Markus Keller left on his motorbike to ride past on the road
and then to report back. They heard his bike return as they
stood watching. He ran across from where he stopped keeping low and hidden from view.

"August Schafer's vehicle has gone. I could see no sign of
movement on your farm Klaus. It was very quiet. To stop
may have alerted them so I simply rode past and then waited
a while and rode back."

The men, Egon Kingele, Klaus Muller, Dieter Falke and
Markus Keller all stood in silence unsure of what to do. They
saw Adriane walking across the fields to join them. She was

holding something black.

"Binoculars. They were in the house when we moved in," she explained to the others. "Perhaps they'll give you a better view."

"Is Hauke at the house?"

She touched her husband's arm.

"He's staying away as instructed. Be patient with him. He's very concerned about Mila and he's terrified that he made the wrong decision."

Dieter was peering through the binoculars.

"Back at our house after you took Hauke inside Ursula agreed to return home and inspect the woods. Still, I have a bad feeling that this is where something may happen. If we have luck on our side we may catch Mila on her way. If she is already there .... I don't know."

He continued to scrutinise the Schroder farm.

"It has just occurred to me," said Egon. He pointed a finger at Klaus Muller. "What type of gun is your shotgun, Klaus?"

"It is a very old but handsome double-barrel weapon. It belonged to my father. Why do you ask?"

"I'd imagine it is very loud?"

"Oh yes, quite a racket when it is fired ......"

"Exactly," said Egon. "If it had been discharged nearby we surely would have heard it. Whatever is happening I don't think a shotgun blast is part of it yet."

Dieter interrupted the conversation.

"Boden Meler just moved from the doorway of your main shed, Walter. He went to the little shed where they sleep. Wait, now he has run back. He was carrying something."

Dieter turned to the others.

"That was not the relaxed gait of a man with no cares.

He was in a panic. Looking about, crouching."
The group lay against the mound that hid them from view.
They took turns to watch with the binoculars. The two men
at the piggery had not returned to their work after lunch.
They had not been seen at all. Were they packing to leave,
plotting, panicking, waiting to be taken away by August Scha-
fer? Where was Mila? Close by, waiting? Already inside? Or
the unthinkable, she was their hostage?
Frozen by indecision they waited and talked. afraid to move.
Some good news emerged when Ilse Schroder and their son
Manfred were seen briefly looking out the house window.
It was decided that they had locked themselves in the house.
It was Adriane who finally suggested a plan of action.
She stood and faced the men, hands on her hips.
"You are all in one place. If they are planning to leave then
they might have arranged transport. Assuming they have
Mila then will they leave her behind, take her with them
as a bargaining piece or they may do her harm. Whatever
happens, it seems to me that all of you bunched together in
one place will not be as effective as if you were spread out,
surrounding the farm, covering all directions."

After her speech, the men looked startled. Everything the
woman said made sense.
Markus said, "Of course." He surveyed the area.
"I'll go to the road."
He began to slide away to move unseen to the fields and to
the road.
Hans Muller stayed his arm.
"If Mila is involved … " He turned to all the group. "We must
do everything to save her."

"Hans," said Dieter, "It's why we're here. It is our only cause. No other matter is of interest."

Egon moved to the rear of the piggery where a dirt track allowed access to the back of the area. It was rugged and unlikely to be used but they wanted to have lookouts on all sides. He had his strongest work boots on his feet. Perfect for the mud he explained.
Walter Schroder wanted to remain at their mound and watch via the binoculars. Adriane would stay with him.
Dieter decided that his best chance of an intercept would be near the road where the new building was half erected.
It was there he considered would be the most likely unobserved pickup point.

With each man out of view of the others the afternoon progressed.
At one point a group of large black birds flew overhead calling occasionally.
Dieter lay in a culvert. He could not name the birds but it pleased him that birds were once again part of the landscape. He would not have blamed all the birds of Europe if they left Germany never to return.
The grass under his shirt was damp but by lifting his head occasionally he could see the doorway of the main shed where Boden Meler had disappeared inside some time back.
He wondered what tactic could be employed if nothing happened and the light began to fade. Perhaps they were waiting for nightfall to make their move. It would render the whole operation much more difficult.
Briefly, he considered the chance of simply walking up to

the building as if nothing was amiss. It was just possible that Mila was not inside, that August Schafer had not been in the area to visit them, that they were unaware of any issues and were just being lazy.

In his persona as the former Hauptsturmführer he would simply chat, check the construction, ask to see Walter, find the man was not at home then bid them a cheerful farewell perhaps adding that he had some business in town.

The idea was quickly dismissed as absurd. Too many factors pointed to there being unusual activity at the building,

His next wish was that Ursula Muller had indeed found a distraught Mila sitting with her back against a tree in their little forest. That she was right now sitting with the girl at their house, talking to her and comforting her, discussing her troubles.

As he lay staring at the sky he wished that whatever the outcome of this day it mark the end of all the past years and the beginning of a new form of life and hope. That was his greatest wish.

His musing was interrupted by the sound of a vehicle approaching. It was only then that he realised there had been no other traffic past all day. Not so unusual on their quiet backroad.

Raising his head he watched the door of the shed. The noise of the vehicle came closer and then suddenly stopped and silence resumed.

Now he was sure. Whatever was about to take place would reveal the true situation.

By sliding a little way along the culvert Dieter was able to view proceedings through a clump of grass. It would make him much less likely to be spotted.

At first, nothing changed then he was aware of a quite bulky man struggling up from the road embankment to the new building framework.

It must be August Schafer. He looked familiar. Perhaps from passing by in the town.

At this moment Boden Meler appeared at the door of the shed. He lifted his hand in recognition. In return the man from the car waved his arm hurriedly, beckoning them on. Meler moved back briefly as if fetching his belongings then came out of the doorway. Over his shoulder was a large canvas sack. Hanging from his right arm was a shotgun.

Dieter started as he saw the gun. Before he could process this information Gerrit Klein followed out the door. He too had a canvas bag over his shoulder. Being pushed and marched in front of him with her face covered by a sack was the girl Mila.

They made their way past the small shed and out toward the new building where their visitor waited.

He had stopped. Now he raised his arms in a motion of calling a halt. He was angry.

"Nein, nein! Ich sagte, das Mädchen zu verlassen. Ich werde sie nicht nehmen."

Dieter stared. He was torn by indecision.

'Leave the girl? He will not take her?' What was happening? Klein snarled back.

"She is our insurance. We will dispose of her later."

"Dann ist unser Arrangement abgesagt."

Dieter's eyes moved between the two parties.

He was 'cancelling' their 'arrangement'.

Boden Meler strode forward to confront the other man.

He was every bit the assured, arrogant Scharfuhrer from the death camp.

"Is that your final word?"

"Ja. Leg das Mädchen zurück oder ich gehe."

Dieter lay watching the events. Who would concede?

"Then we no longer need you," said Meler.

For a moment the scene hung as if stilled by the tension of the confrontation, then it all ended.

With a smack of sound in the silent afternoon, the shotgun discharged and the man August Schafer flew backwards and flopped to the ground. He lay still in the dirt.

Boden Meler leaned down searching the dead man's pockets. Mila could be seen shaking. Klein wrenched her arms upward. Her wrists were tied at the back.

"The keys must be in the car."

The two men grabbed each side of the girl and began almost lifting her as they marched her forward toward the embankment.

It was time to act. Dieter prayed that Boden Meler may be distracted, may have some vestige of respect for the man Dieter had pretended to be, anything that would make him discharge his remaining shot badly. He stood.

At first, they did not notice him. He decided to speak while still at a distance.

"Boden, Gerrit," he called. "Boden Gerrit!"

They jumped and swung around.

"What in hell?"

Dieter Falke cupped his hands and called out.

"This will not work. Time to stop. You can go if you release the girl. You know it's sensible. It's my best and only offer. I can't let you leave with her."

It was Klein who almost rose from the ground in anger and indignation. He swung Mila round as roughly as he could holding her by the neck, lifting her up.

"You lying swine. We believed you. We believed in you. You were somebody that we could respect …. Now it's time to pay. You will see …… "

He seemed to be distressed. To Dieter, his voice took on the tone of a snivelling brat.

"The war is over. We lost the war. There are consequences, Gerrit. You must know that."

Boden Meler raised the shotgun.

"We're going now. You liar, you fraud. This little bitch came to kill us. Apparently, we didn't get all of her family. Do not come near or you'll suffer the fate of this dead fool here on the ground."

The threesome began moving forward once more, making their way to the embankment and the car.

Dieter wanted to rush in, to take a chance that he would be missed but this was a shotgun. At best he would be wounded. Thus no use to anybody. Still, he considered his chances. Once the shot was fired the gun was empty. Did they have more shells? He doubted the girl would have thought to bring spare cartridges. He needed to be close enough to attack them. There was a risk they would harm the girl if he didn't get to them in time.

A voice came from below. They stopped. A man was yelling from the roadway. Dieter stopped. It was Markus.

"You can't shoot all of us, fellow. You are not going to leave. I have the keys to the car and I have even disabled the motor. Stop now. Do you hear me? Stop now!”

The two men with the girl seemed lost in a sea of indecision. They stepped forward then back like a car with gearbox fault.
A hurried discussion was taking place. Angry words spat from their mouths. They glared across the field at Dieter. He called to them again just as Markus appeared at the top of the embankment then ducked back as he saw the gun. “Please gentlemen, the war is over. It is time to make things right. Justice will prevail. It will be fair. Don’t stain your lives further with some futile act. Let the girl walk to me.”
To his left Dieter caught movement. Klaus Muller had emerged from behind the mound. He stood with his arms out.
“Mila,” he called, imploringly.
The girl’s head swung in the direction of his voice. She cried out. Words they could not understand from beneath her hood. The exchange seemed to create a tipping point for the two Scharfuhrers.
Klein put his arm around Mila’s neck and began dragging her backwards almost choking her in his rush. Meler was also walking backwards swinging the shotgun from side to side, providing cover.
“You want the girl? Come and get her. We’ll be waiting.For the glory of the Reich you traitors. Come and get this girl. See the consequences of your actions. It is you who have brought this on yourselves and now it is time for you to pay. Come, take your precious daughter of a non-believer …….”
Meler’s rant continued as they reached the doorway of the main building and disappeared inside.

His voice could still be heard from within though they could
no longer understand his challenge.

Egon came stumbling toward the three men standing near
the small shed.
Klaus Muller was in tears.
"They are going to murder the dear girl I know it."
Dieter tried to reassure him.
"If they do then they have no advantage. No card to play in
an attempt to get away."
He only half believed his words. These men were fanatics.
He feared they saw one last act of savagery and glorious
death as a fitting end to the confrontation.
"We can't wait," Dieter advised. "Tell me, Klaus, what sort of
shot is in those shotgun shells? Would it be lethal?"
The man puzzled for a moment.
"The gun was used for ducks and other birds. Small pellets.
It would be lethal at close range but there's no choke. The
spread is wide. Only wounding past a short distance."
"Then," said Dieter, "I'm going to enter the building. If as I
hope they are at the far end then I have a good chance.
We need to know what hope there is of a peaceful outcome."
They walked to the doorway. Lights were on inside.
"What's in this building, Walter?"
"Food for the pigs, a workshop and tools. This building is
under-utilised. Largely empty."
Dieter stepped up to the door. The other men made half-ges-
tures to try to stop him but did not follow through.
He called at the door.
"Boden, Gerrit. I would like to come in. I want to talk to you."
They replied immediately.

"Yes, traitor. By all means, do come in. We would like you all
to come in. See what we think of you, see what happens to
traitors of their country."

Dieter stepped through the door, ready to leap sideways if he
saw the shotgun pointed at him. It took him some seconds
the comprehend what scene awaited him.

The two men were seated at the far end of the big, high
ceilinged room. Boden Meler was perched on several sacks
of grain. He held Mila by the neck, her hands still tied behind
her back. The bag was still over her head.

They had stripped the child's shirt from her body exposing
her boy-like chest. She whimpered quietly. Gerrit Klein was
seated next to her on a single grain sack. He held something
silver in his hand close to her skin. He smiled at Dieter and
held up the tubular object.

"A demonstration for you. Not ideal. We've had to make do.
This, for instance, is for injecting pigs. We found a suitable
long thin tube and attached it. The content is not phenol but
it's a phenolic type of disinfectant. Unfortunately, her death
will be slow and agonising still it's the best we can do."

Dieter felt his face burning. There was simply no way he
could reach them to wrestle and perhaps save the girl.

The distance was too great.

Klein continued his little speech.

"We have discussed this. Of course, we would have preferred
to leave town and then simply slit this girl's throat and drop
her by the road. Now you have ruined that. Instead of a
quick death, it will be ……… more fitting."

He paused and smirked. Gave an odd laugh.

"Do you know she wanted to kill us. Imagine that. She knew,
thanks to you, all about how we disposed of her parents and

her brother and sister. She conveniently explained how we had missed her and that now she would take revenge. Then ……."

He laughed again. Sniggered as if highly amused.

"She couldn't do it! We simply took the gun from her. Hopeless. Now we can complete our job and finish the last of this traitorous family. Who knows, once we're done we may still leave. We have the gun after all.

So …. please, have everybody come in. We would not want anybody to miss this event. A special demonstration by two professional members of the glorious Schutzstaffel Einsatzgruppen. Come, come all those waiting in anticipation.

This is a once in a lifetime opportunity. This is history."

Dieter turned to whisper that under no circumstances were those outside to enter. It would allow these two madmen to carry out their murder with their audience in place.

To his horror Egon, Klaus and Walter were already standing behind him watching the whole procedure. Behind them, Markus also looked on.

"Why did you come in?" he snarled.

Gerrit Klein was already talking once more.

"Good, good. No use delaying proceedings. Please watch carefully. I may be a little imperfect. I am out of practice but the result will be just as dramatic."

"Oh God," thought Dieter, "he's going to do it."

What Dieter remembered next was a sharp crack very close to his ear. As he lurched sideways away from the noise he was aware of Gerrit Klein spinning round and falling from his seat.

He swapped his points of view from the men in the doorway to the scene at the other end. The fine barrel of a gun was sitting on Walter Schroder's shoulder. Directly behind him holding the rifle was Markus Keller. He was rushing to place another cartridge into the chamber.

Back at the other end, Gerrit Klein was writhing on the floor holding his arm. The large needle was on the floor away from him.

Boden Meler was screaming obscenities. He rose, holding Mila round the neck, her body shielding him.

Markus Keller was saying, I can't get a shot. I can't get a shot."

Now Boden Meler was holding a shining field issue knife to his side. He brought it up to Mila's neck. He was screaming. "You won't win, you fools. All your plans, your stupid plots. Watch her die."

All the men at the doorway froze, their eyes wide, their fears as one focused on the impossible horrible truth of what was about to happen.

A small figure rose from behind the sacks of grain. He held aloft a long-handled shovel. One of the very shovels used to dig the foundations of the new shed.

As Boden Meler, his eyes wide in triumph brought the blade of his knife to the soft, gentle skin of Mila's neck, Hauke brought his shovel down, with all the force his small frame was capable of achieving, onto the head of Boden Meler.

The man simply fell sideways in an ugly, undignified collapse. Hauke reached out and hugged the girl as tightly as he could. He cried a rasping, desperate cry and under the cloth of her hood, Mila cried out and repeated his name over and over.

Chapter 34

'The Americans'

Hans Koch placed the call to the American base. Only after the Americans were on their way did he walk two streets to the Stadtpolizei office and inform them of the events that had taken place.
The man he saw, sighed, made a note of the information in the daily log and then closed the book before the ink was dry. He looked at Hans.
"Thank you for your courtesy. You must know we can do little other than control traffic and try to wear our uniforms to look reassuring. Still, if anybody asks we have it all on record. The Americans will take care of matters for you I'm sure."
He smiled his wan smile and indicated to the door. The official part of the matter was concluded.

A lot happened during the day.

Mila was taken away from the scene before Klaus removed the hood from her head. It was his way of sparing her any additional trauma. She was quiet but she would not let go of Hauke. Perhaps it was her need to have something she knew and understood to cling onto. Klaus fussed over her and kissed her cheek repeatedly.

Walter Schroder brought his truck round and transported Klaus and the girl complete with attached boy, back to the Muller farm so that she could be cared for completely, away from the recent drama.

Adriane considered her options. It was Dieter who looked at his tired, distraught wife and suggested a course of action.

"I forget myself sometimes. My love for you suggests that you should go to our house and rest. For your sake and the sake of the child, you are soon to bring into this world. I will be back with our boy very soon and we'll sit for a minute and thank destiny that we are together."

Adriane reached up and kissed her husband's cheek.

He watched her walking back across the fields before turning his attention to current matters.

The two captives had their feet tied together. A bandage was placed over the split on Boden Meler's head and his hands were fastened behind his back. He groaned and complained that his skull was surely broken but gained no sympathy.

Gerrit Klein had a clear hole through his upper right arm. The bullet may have grazed the bone. It oozed blood.

He held it to his chest, rocking backward and forward from the pain. A rope was placed around his wrists then round his chest to lock his arms in place.

Except for the occasional expletive or reference to God in

relation to their pain, neither man spoke to their captors. Their bravado was gone and with it went any need for arrogance or justification of their deeds and cause.

All the men involved in the confrontation were as one amazed and grateful that a seemingly hopeless situation resolved itself in such a positive manner.
Certain actions were taken after discussion, in order to set up the scene for the Americans.
An ancient pitted and rusted shotgun was found by Walter along with a souvenir WWI pistol. The shotgun they would say was used to slay August Schafer and the pistol was the weapon that stopped Herr Klein from his murderous action.
Dieter looked at the two weapons.
"The Americans are not fools. These pieces of equipment are barely serviceable, in fact, dangerous to the user I suspect. I doubt they will believe they are the weapons used in this incident."
"Even so," replied Walter. "If they are fair-minded they may overlook the obvious subterfuge and focus on the bigger picture. I would not like to see them confiscate the heirloom shotgun from Klaus or take away the fine weapon that Markus has hidden.

Earlier Markus had given them some background to his days in the war.
He was a late conscript. Drawn into the Wehrmacht, his past record in target shooting labelled him immediately as a potential sniper. He was given a Mauser K98 with a scope and put through training. He excelled. At war's end, he was fighting in Germany against the rapidly advancing Russian's.

"I only ever killed Russians," he said. "I preferred it that way."

When it became obvious that the war was lost and only futility and death awaited those who remained he followed many of his comrades and took the chance to just fade away.

The Russians did not like snipers and made sure they suffered a slow and terrible death. So he threw away his beloved rifle. He then exchanged clothes with a fallen soldier and became a lowly ranked regular soldier. Like Dieter, he realised that the Russians would be vengeful conquerors so he made his way back to his home. To Willingen. Inside the American zone.

"I know this part of the country quite well. I was able to avoid both the Russians and the Americans."

"Where did you obtain the rifle you used just now?" asked Dieter.

"It's my old target rifle. With a nice scope its extremely accurate. I still have the licence to own such a weapon, if it's valid. I don't wish to ask."

"Let us hope the Americans don't send a suspicious officer who sticks to the rules."

"Yes, we must hope for that."

Two large trucks with canvas-covered backs arrived together with a US Army staff car.

A large number of US soldiers jumped out of the trucks and moved up the embankment across the farm, past all the pig pens and buildings to quickly encircle the area. Only then did the staff car drive in through the farm entrance gate and come to a halt where the men were standing. The driver did not alight. Three other men did. Two were officers, followed by a man in a suit.

By some default, it was Dieter who moved forward to be the spokesman. The man in the suit addressed him in fluent German.

"I'm Harold Jessop. I'm attached to US Army Intelligence charged with prosecuting war criminals. Can I suggest we find a place to sit down? I like to be in possession of all the facts and all the story in every case. It has been my experience with examination of accusations of war crimes that if the discussion is allowed to run free it can be very confusing and we lose track of what exactly we are being told and what parts of the story fit into what time frame. You understand?" The man was not unpleasant however he explained he worked on facts, not hearsay.

Walter Schroder suggested the adjourn to the house kitchen. "Can the prisoners be guarded?" he asked the man Jessop.

"They already are," replied the man.

What seemed to the men would be a straight-forward procedure where the two prisoners were handed over to the Americans proved more complex.

They were asked many questions and the hand-written notes that they had presumed would be sufficient evidence formed only part of the case against the two Auschwitz operatives. There were witnesses to be found and sworn statements from survivors. A detailed account of the events that had occurred that day was taken down and then they all had to sign the paperwork to guarantee its veracity.

The man in the suit was a law court prosecutor and worked to a legal system that required facts.

They had coffee and biscuits and worked on until the Americans were satisfied that they had the amount of detail, evidence and background to hold and prosecute the prisoners. All names were taken so that when the case was brought to the military tribunals dealing with the death camps certain persons may be required to attend to bear witness and give their story.

"Understand, please. Germany is a damaged country. It is physically damaged but there is also an undercurrent of anger, confusion and revenge that equates to mental damage. We must be cautious. Not all cases are as they seem. Many involve false testimony and doubtful claims. We have to be sure if we are to be seen to be administering genuine justice.

Military Police arrived. They were taken to the prisoners whereby the two American officers ordered their MPs to escort the men, via a medical facility, to the US Army holding prison.

As they were marched away Gerrit Klein stared at Dieter.

"You have betrayed two fellow Germans. Have you no shame?"

Dieter looked back at the angry, hateful man.

"You betrayed yourself and Germany by your actions. Don't try to apportion blame to others. Your decisions and your part in this were all your own. Our country must live with your crimes."

Photographs were taken of the area, the final scene and the body of August Schafer.

When the soldier photographer came to photograph the alleged weapons used in the incident he shook his head and was about to speak to one of the officers. The man directed him back to his task.

"I know. I know, Just take the photographs. It's of no consequence."

The man shrugged and made his shot..

An undertaker brought from the town arrived in his van and
loaded the corpse in the back.

The man whispered to Egon.

"What happened here? Who shot August?"

"I can't talk now."

"His wife will be annoyed."

"Annoyed?"

"That's about all. He wasn't a nice man. Some said he beat
her. Is this to do with the two SS chaps?"

He stood looking at Egon expectantly. He was a man who
provided a service for those who had departed life but also
a gossip. No doubt recent years had provided a great deal of
custom for such a business. The interesting news that often
accompanied a death would be seen as a bonus.

Egon was called away. He and Dieter and Markus were taken
in the staff car to the Muller's orchards to see and speak with
Klaus and Ursula Muller and then with Mila.

All that the men had told the Americans was corroborated
by the interviews.

The man in the suit seemed satisfied. In an out of character
moment, he took Dieter and Egon aside.

"I can't imagine what that girl Mila has just gone through.
She was reasonably coherent considering her ordeal.
I noticed she did not let go of the boy's hand at any stage.
At times she squeezed it so tight that he was in pain yet he

said nothing. It will take a community to help her get over it all. Her young friend Hauke may be the key."

Harold Jessop smiled briefly.

"That is all for now. You'll be kept posted. Please be ready for when you are called."

"When might that be?" asked Dieter.

The American picked up his satchel full of papers.

"There's quite a list. From our current workload, up to two years."

Chapter 35

'The Days That Followed'

Dieter Falke climbed a ladder onto the roof of his barn.
He said it was to check the shingles and make any repairs.
The day produced a light, cool breeze. The sky was mostly
blue with remnant clouds idling by. In the yard, Adriane went
about placing a few items on their washing line. By starting
early they should dry by days end.
The man on the roof watched his wife. She would very soon
give birth to their child. He trembled slightly, overcome with
the oddity of repetition. It was from this vantage point that
he had watched the arrival, the rebirth of their boy. Watched
Adriane run to greet him. At that time and ever since he was
at peace and swelled with love for his family. A collection of
three orphans. Leftover debris from a mad, dysfunctional
world. His life had a second beginning. He hoped his ascent

this morning would add strength to those feelings. Bring forth even greater satisfaction. It was not necessary but like a drug addict, he felt that one more hit could do no harm. So he lay down, placed his hands behind his head and looked up to stare at the sky. It rarely produced waves anymore of black specs racing to and fro. There were only occasional planes now. They seemed to be pacing themselves when they appeared as if their journey was routine rather than vital.

Almost a month had passed since the drama at the Schroder's farm. The process of evaluating feelings and finding a degree of calm was ongoing.
Walter Schroder would not consider having any other strangers working at his piggery despite needing help and there being many people looking for work. The situation resolved itself when Manfred Schroder announced that he would forego his immediate ambitions to pursue an academic future and would put all his efforts into helping his father. This led to a rekindling of the father-son relationship and the two spent much time together discussing all manner of worldly topics. Both parties were surprised at how much they each knew about so many things.

An arrangement formed between Lena and Hans Koch and the Keller family whereby the children, Dolph and Gerde, would proceed to the Post Office after school each day and spend time being cared for until their mother Antje called by after finishing work to take them home. Having the children in safe hands meant that Antje could work more hours and supplement their income.

The children loved being spoiled by the two postal people and were allowed to help out at the front counter. The facade that Lena and Hans so carefully tended over the years as two rather conservative, stern adults began to melt. They were often seen to laugh nowadays and customers found them quite pleasant.

Egon Kingele spent even more time visiting the Falke farm. His casual calls became such that although no indications were ever made as to his standing, it was accepted that he had assumed the role of the family grandfather and thus he was part of the daily routine.
His now jovial nature brought calm to everyday affairs. Also, it was no secret that he eagerly awaited the birth of the new child.
He could spend a lot of time sitting in the sun with Hauke while they talked on a range of things. When they finished both seemed fulfilled by the experience. Dieter often watched them and wondered what the conversation entailed. He never asked. His dealings with Hauke were that of a father and his son. It was a level he now delighted in pursuing. They joked about, talked heroically, even wrestled playfully.
A bond that at last was established and now held.
Martha Kingele continued her quest to teach Adriane all that she knew about cooking and producing hearty meals. Both houses were filled with interesting aromas which considering ongoing rations were quite astounding.
"You've been seeing that Martha woman again," Dieter would say with a wink as his wife placed something truly delicious on his plate.

"Oma Martha does magical things," added Hauke.

"So it's Oma now is it?" Adriane queried.

"Do you think she'd mind? I've never had a grandmother."

"I think she would be delighted. Why don't you try Vater on Egon as well. That will make him very happy."

At the Muller's orchards there existed a tense calm. Following her ordeal at the hands of the SS men, those that knew all the details were collectively concerned for Mila. They convinced themselves that there would be consequences. It was not possible, they espoused, to go through such an event without ongoing mental anguish. There had to be psychological damage.

The girl was watched most closely.

It was true that for a week after her rescue Mila spent a great deal of time in bed. While Klaus and Ursula Muller tended to her needs, fed her and loved her she seemed largely untroubled by all that had happened. Her demeanour was quiet but detached. Subjects for conversation were far removed from her near-death encounter or the fate of her parents and siblings.

This, of course, worried the Mullers even more. They waited for signs they felt would at some stage overwhelm the girl and she would completely break down. They were sure this would happen. They told their neighbours as much. They could only wait and be ready. What would be the catalyst?

Mila liked to sit and read to her little half-brother.

They would often be found asleep with the girl holding the young boy like a comforting teddy bear.

Above all, there remained one person who seemed to have

her confidence. Hauke visited Mila every day. They were left alone to talk, to be together, to hold hands, to just exist. Mila was always especially quiet after Hauke's visits. It seemed she drew strength from his presence. He was the only person of her age that she knew who had suffered as much as her. On one visit while Klaus and Ursula Muller sat in their kitchen Mila appeared in the doorway from the hall with Hauke.

"Oh," said Ursula, "You're dressed. How nice my dear."

"We're going outside for a walk."

Ursula rose and gave both the young pair a hug and a kiss on the cheek.

"That sounds like a wonderful idea. Some nice fresh air. The type you can only find outside."

After they had gone she looked at her husband.

"What an odd thing for me to say. About the air .... "

"You were excited. I wonder where they've gone?"

They carefully pulled aside the window curtain trying not to be caught and spoil the moment.

Mila and Hauke were walking up a slight rise in one of the orchards. The dappled light flickered over their backs as they passed under each tree. Near the top of the field, they stopped and sat down almost out of sight under one of the apple trees. Their backs could just be seen. As they settled in only their heads remained visible.

From where they sat they would have been able to see the Kingele's farm and further away, the top of the hill with part of the Falke's' farm and the road that wound into the distance off to the Muller's piggery.

"He's a clever boy, that Hauke. We couldn't budge her from her bed."

Klaus took one more look before leaving the window.
"Whatever is happening perhaps just talking about everyday
things will give our Mila a little help. Time can heal to some
extent. I suppose it depends on the severity of what may be
recalled or forgotten."

It was more than that. As they sat shoulder to shoulder
against the tree Hauke decided in his thirteen-year-old mind
that the subject must be tackled, not kindly and thoughtfully
avoided.
Perhaps he was right.
"Mila," he began, "I've told you everything it is possible to
tell about me and you've told me the same about you. We
know all there is to know about each other except ....
I don't know how you felt at Herr Schroder's shed. Where
you were about to die. Where we all prayed that no harm
would come to you but all seemed sure you were going to be
killed by stabbing your heart with a needle.
That is not something you hide away and not talk about.
Anymore than knowing the fate of your parents and your
brother and sister. I'm your friend. I want you to tell me you
were scared. Tell me you thought all hope was lost. Tell me
all your secret thoughts. Because I was terrified so you must
have been also. I need to know my dearest Mila. Tell me.
Please tell me."
Mila looked at the face of the boy next to her. His eyes were
red. This hero, this boy who saved her. He wanted to know.
Of course. Nobody had asked before.
She looked into his strange eyes. Her very own angel. She
turned herself to face him silently putting her arms around
his neck and holding him with her head on his shoulder.

It was then that it all happened. From a blank canvas in her mind, the whole wretched ordeal flooded her consciousness. Every moment ran through her like lightning through her veins. She was there again. It was happening all over. Hidden in darkness inside that hood breathing frantically. Yes, she felt the razor tip of that needle touch her chest. Felt the rope around her wrists. She heard the conversations, the pleas, uncontrolled raving of madmen, the gunshot, the screaming, the chaos, all unknown in her darkness. From nowhere that thud and then nobody was holding her. Then Hauke's voice next to her ear. It was all there and she could not keep it in anymore.

She let out a deep anguished moan. Not loud but extended as if an animal escaped her lips. She lowered her head onto the boy's chest and as he cradled her and caressed her she cried and shook and broke away from it all, putting it in a place where it would become a part of her past. Thus she stayed for near half an hour. Sighing at times. Slowing, subsiding, finding her way back.

At the end when she no longer shook and her breathing became easy Hauke leaned down close to her ear just as he had done on that day. This time he whispered ....

"Thank you. Thank you for telling me."

They sat together for another hour and talked through all of her short life. She allowed the descriptions of her family's death to be explored and understood. They processed every moment of her attempt to take revenge on the two murderers and how at the crucial time when she could have fired the gun she instead found that she could not take another human life. How instead she was captured and seemed doomed to suffer the same fate as the rest of her family. To complete the horrible destruction that started years before. It was Hauke who pointed out how her survival was a triumph against the system that condemned the rest of her family. She had won and thus remained the link that those evil men could not destroy.

He was quite proud of the eloquence of his words and the effect they seemed to have on his friend. She was engaged with the world again. If she could talk about the events that changed her life she would cope. Their world was still there to be lived in and explored. It lay ahead of them.

The town was a place that all these families initially feared. Would they be understood? Handing over two German soldiers to the enemy. How would such actions be interpreted? Despite many townspeople attending Dieter's reports concerning the situation he still was uneasy. Trips to the town were approached for a short time with trepidation. Nothing obvious came to light but still, they waited for some hostility. Except for the people who ran the post office.

Hans and Lena Koch took a different approach. They placed photos of the two Scharfuhrers above their counter with the words -

> **'These criminals who murdered German citizens**
> **and children are now to face justice.**
> **Please sign the paper on our counter to show your**
> **support for the actions taken by your fellow citizens.'**

Within two weeks Hans Koch calculated that over 90% of the

people of Willingen had signed the papers. It seemed that German loyalty and pride was superseded by the actions of Meler and Klein. Even in war there were limits to barbarity.

The farms around Dieter and Adriane were all in full production. While each was a small landholding, they worked hard and in a ruined country still struggling to emerge from its devastation their produce would readily sell. The US Army paid good money to feed its troops but most farmers took a lesser amount for much of their output to ensure that local people could eat a decent meal.
Even Dieter Falke the young man from Dresden who studied to be an engineer became a reasonable farmer. His efforts were applauded by his neighbours.

At night he would often sit on his favourite lounge chair and read a book. A whole room in the living quarters at the Post Office was full of books. It seemed Hans and Lena Koch had a passion for the printed word. They were equally passionate about seeing others reading and so the room became a must-visit place for Dieter, Adriane and Hauke on every trip to the town.
Hauke would often forego the shopping when they called in and stay sitting cross-legged on the floor absorbed in some volume he had found.
Hans Koch whispered to his wife one day as they noticed the boy, "If we'd ever had a son, I do believe he may have been the one."
She smiled gently and kissed his cheek and they moved away to leave the reader in peace.

Dieter would occasionally pause in his reading. Alone, with the others asleep a wash of emotions would sweep over him. All the life he had lived so far came up in patches of memory. Should he be content? Was a life such as this a blessing or simply a refuge from all the sorrow and horror that had gone before?
Were they fortunate or simply the shattered remains of other lives and other times, thrown together to make a mockery of a family?
His feelings were raw and his thoughts at times produced incredible sadness. So much so that he would look about the room to be sure he remained alone.

Eventually, he would rise and make his way to his bed.
He would lay down beside his wife and look at her face at peace and asleep. He too would drift into sleep.
In the morning he would rise once more and discover that the daylight had returned, that his wife and son would greet him happily at the breakfast table and the earth and the fields out of his window continued to grow new life.

AFTER

Scharführer Gerrit Klein and Scharführer Boden Meler were initially
held by the United States Army branch in Germany, while investi-
gations into their alleged war crimes took place. During checking
and clarification of the allegations made against the two men, the
Supreme National Tribunal of Poland, based in Warsaw, became
aware that the two men were in custody.
With extensive files on Klein and Meler they placed a formal
request with the US authorities that the men be handed over to
the Tribunal to stand trial.
After an exchange of paperwork, it was agreed by the US Army
that custody be formally granted to Poland and both prisoners
were duly transferred to Warsaw a month later.
The Supreme National Tribunal of Poland immediately added Klein
and Meler to their list awaiting prosecution.

While being held in a prison on the outskirts of the Polish capital
a man entered their cell holding his keys and carrying a large tray
with their evening meal. From under his tray, the man produced a

medium-sized axe while at the same time kicking the door closed
to shut off access for the guard. The man then proceeded to attack
the cell's occupants. Such was the ferocity of the attack that both
men sustained terrible injuries to their faces, hands and upper
bodies.
At this point, the man stopped.
Guards eventually managed to unlock the door once more.
The two prisoners lay on the cell floor groaning in agony while
their attacker sat and watched.
He told the guards, "They killed our children. Please, let them die
slowly."

Scharführer Boden Meler died two days later in the prison hospital. Scharführer Gerrit Klein spent another five days in great pain
before he too passed away. Unconfirmed reports suggest that only
minimal pain relief was said to have been administered to both
men during their time in the hospital, although this would have
been in direct violation of the Geneva Convention.

Josef Klehr, the man who invented the phenol injection method
used at Auschwitz was released by the Americans in 1948.
He returned to his home town of Braunschweig to resume a
normal life. It was not until 1960 that any further action was taken
against him. This time by a German court.
He died at his home in 1988 aged 83.

Five weeks after the events at the Schroder piggery Adriane Falke
delivered a healthy baby girl. They named her Mia.

Hauke's scar has now faded to a faint line. He does not consider it
dramatic enough to bother showing people anymore.

Hauke Falke and Mila Muller remain very close friends.
Both were officially adopted by their respective families.
They spend a lot of time reading books together.
When they walk through the town and hold hands, people whisper
and smile.